DARKEST BEFORE YOU DIE

DARKEST BEFORE YOU DIE

A HORROR SHORT STORY COLLECTION

MARK ALLEN

Darkest Before You Die: A Horror Short Story Collection
Paperback Edition
Copyright © 2025 by Mark Allen

Dark Wolf Books
An Imprint of Wolfpack Publishing
1707 E. Diana Street
Tampa, FL 33610

www.darkwolfbooks.com

Edited by My Brother's Editor

Paperback ISBN 979-8-89567-904-3
Ebook ISBN 979-8-89567-903-6
LCCN 2025945508

CONTENTS

Jarin's Song   1
Naïveté   22
Prey   24
Shafted   45
Sacred Creed   54
Sanity's Twitch   56
Suck A Bus   64
Armageddon's Gallows   101
Chance Dance   103
Broken Mirror   116
The Patriot   129
The Desecration   135
The Razor's Voice   137
Golgotha's Wine   142
An Honest Mistake   147
Fallen Angel, Risen Dove   163
Love(?)   177
All The Way   179
Worse Than Death   188

A Look At: Gateways to Annihilation:
Stories   223
About the Author   225

DARKEST BEFORE YOU DIE

JARIN'S SONG

AUTHOR'S NOTE

Psychoanalyze my writing, especially the short stuff, and you'll unearth a recurring theme of desperate souls suffering horribly as they seek to be loved. Believe it or not, "Jarin's Song" was inspired by the cheesy music video for Twisted Sister's "We're Not Gonna Take It." What began as a story about a rebellious teenage wannabe rock star morphed into a twisted tale of a handicapped kid, his abusive father, and just how far someone will go to find acceptance.

Jarin Harper's fingers blistered the strings of his electric guitar as he played along to Twisted Sister's "We're Not Gonna Take It." The amp screamed out metallic thunder as lead vocalist Dee Snider snarled from the rack of speakers connected to the stereo. Twisted Sister was one of his favorite bands, classic rebel rock from the '80s, and he loved playing his guitar to their tunes. He knew every song by heart and could reproduce the entire *Stay Hungry* album lick by delicious lick.

These are the kinds of hooks you can hang a tune on, he thought. *Not like today's rock. Nowadays you don't even have to play well, just make a lot of noise, throw on some auto-tune, and bam! You're a modern rock star.*

As his fingers danced across the guitar, wringing out wrenching, bombastic music from the thrumming strings, his eyes flicked to the drum set squatting in the corner of the room. He saw the dust coating the skins, and bitterness welled up inside him. Before the accident, drums had been his instrument of choice, for rock was based on beat. Rock without rhythm was an oxymoron, like a zoo without animals. The two were inextricably linked, and it was this singular facet of rock that had drawn him to the drums when he was four, banging away on pots and pans until Mom, God rest her soul, finally broke down and bought him a Fisher Price drum set. The tiny trailer they'd lived in at the time had rock-and-rolled to the erratic, out-of-time beats of a child drummer until the neighbors had begged for mercy.

By fifteen, he was an accomplished drummer. He and his friends, Marcus and Dave, formed their own band, playing gigs here and there, belting out cover tunes from AC/DC, Aerosmith, and Cinderella. They had been on their way to stardom, no doubt about it.

Then came the dare.

Then the accident.

Then the dream ended.

Whoever said God protects fools was a damn liar. He

continued to play, his fingers flying over the strings. A new song now played, Snider screaming about wanting to rock. Jarin's guitar wailed as he remembered that dark day two years ago when he, Marcus, and Dave had played the fools. Didn't seem fair that he was the only one who paid for it, but he wouldn't wish his fate on anyone, let alone his two best friends. Well, former best friends. Simple fact was, Marcus and Dave got lucky. He didn't. End of story.

A new beat intruded into the music, pulling his attention back to the present. For a moment he thought his CD player was skipping, then he realized the beat wasn't a drum but the sound of someone pounding on his bedroom door. "Hey!" his father yelled. "What the hell do you call that noise in there?"

Twisted Sister snarled, *"I wanna—"*

"ROCK!" Jarin shouted with the band.

"Yeah?" his father shouted back. "I'm gonna rock your head if you don't turn that shit down!"

Jarin bit down on the "Screw you!" that rose to his lips—his old man was always nagging him about his music—and settled for slamming the strings, causing a blast of electrified guitar to howl from the amplifier.

"Did you hear me, Jarin? I said turn it down!"

"Yeah, I heard you. So what?" Jarin muttered. He knew his dad couldn't hear him over the music's roar. He blistered the strings again. The windows rattled in their frames.

His door flew open, replaced by the angry figure of Gary Harper. Jarin looked into his father's eyes, saw the hazel was flecked with crimson highlights, and knew he was in trouble. Those red motes never appeared in his dad's eyes unless he was really pissed.

"Did you hear me say turn that shit down?" Gary snarled.

"Wasn't sure what you said."

"Don't you dare lie to me, boy. I will yank you right out of that wheelchair and beat the sass out of you."

Jarin's next words shot from his lips before he could catch them. "Takes a real tough guy to beat up on a kid with no legs."

The motes in his father's eyes began to swirl like debris caught in a savage whirlpool. A flush crept across his cheeks. "What did you say to me?" he demanded, his voice low, deceptively soft. He may as well have asked, "How was your day at school, son?"

Jarin had rolled the dice of defiance and decided he might as well stick to his guns. "You heard me," he said.

"Yeah, I guess I did." As Twisted Sister growled about burning in Hell, Gary strode over to the stereo and punched his fist through one of the speakers.

"Are you crazy?" Jarin yelled. "Those speakers are five hundred bucks a piece!"

"And all you play on them is this heavy metal crap." Gary punched out the other speaker, silencing the music.

"That's my damn business!"

"Watch your mouth when you talk to me, boy."

"You're buying me new speakers."

"I ain't doing dick. I'm the boss around here, not you. 'Bout time you learned that, son."

"Take your 'son' and shove it, *Dad*." Jarin sneered the endearment into an obscenity, then angrily riffed the guitar strings. Nothing came out of the ruined speakers, but the strings still made a cacophonic buzz-saw noise that bounced defiantly off the walls.

Gary grabbed for the guitar. "Give me that."

"Leave me alone."

"Give it to me."

"Fuck you."

Gary's hand whipped across Jarin's face with a sharp crack. "Say that again, and I swear to God I'll beat you within an inch of your worthless life."

Jarin's face stung like hell. The blow had been hard enough to cut the inside of his cheek against his teeth. He leaned forward in his wheelchair and slowly, deliberately, spat out a mouthful of blood, then looked up at his dad. "Fuck. You."

Gary's hand shot out, grabbed a handful of Jarin's hair, and yanked him out of the wheelchair. It was a bit of a struggle—sitting in a wheelchair had made Jarin a bit pudgy—but Gary got it done. "You mouthy little brat, I'll teach you to talk to me like that."

Jarin hit the floor hard. The carpet scuffed his stinging face like sandpaper. For a moment, he forgot about his disability and tried to stand. He wondered how pathetic he looked, leg stumps wiggling in a pitiful attempt to support him. Self-loathing burned through him like acidic bile, momentarily overpowering his hate for and fear of his father...

...who grabbed the guitar by the neck and raised it over his head like an axe. "Kiss this piece of junk goodbye," Gary said, then slammed it on the floor. The guitar shattered. Strings stretched and popped like severed tendons in the jaws of a hungry wolf. Debris shot everywhere like shrapnel.

"No..." Jarin moaned. He felt pain and a sharp sense of loss, not dissimilar to the loss he felt when he lost his legs. He'd saved for almost a year to buy that guitar, had spent so much time playing it, he felt like it was a part of him. Watching his father ram the mangled guitar through the amp was like having one of his arms torn off.

Gary ripped the wreckage of the guitar free of the amplifier. Only the neck of the instrument remained whole; the rest hung in smashed pieces. The snapped strings dangled to the floor like the lashes of a cat-o'-nine-tails. "There," he said. "That'll teach you to mess with me."

Jarin was ashamed to find himself crying, but he couldn't help it. He felt like he had just lost one of his best friends. "Yeah," he said, voice bristling with fury, "you sure taught me good, you son of a bitch."

The red motes in his dad's eyes started to swirl again, spurred by Jarin's defiance. "Still got some sass left in ya, boy? I got just the cure for that." He stomped his foot down on the back of Jarin's neck, pinning his face to the floor, and began scourging him with the shattered guitar.

Jarin sucked in his breath as the steel strings sliced through his shirt like scalpels and savaged his back. He tried to detach himself from the pain, but it was useless. He heard himself sobbing and felt wet heat running down the curve of his spine as his father flailed away in a mad rage.

Merciful blackness eventually took him, so he never knew how long the beating lasted, but at some point, he awoke from his numbness to find himself face down in his bedroom, alone, the floor and furniture around him speckled with blood. It took him a few moments to realize it was his blood. Took a few more moments for the pain to kick in. But when it did, it kicked like a rabid mule.

He dragged himself over to his desk, ugly leg stumps trailing behind, making him feel like a loathsome slug. He reached up, pulled down a piece of paper and pencil, and began writing a song, some of the words blurred by blood and tears.

———

Wounds heal, but scars remain. That is one of life's cold, hard truths.

Months later, Jarin sat at his computer, face lit by the monitor's glow. He had transferred his song to the hard drive the morning after that hellish night, though he had saved the original sheet of paper on which the song had been born. He didn't know why, but he didn't want to lose the memories, however painful, contained in that blood-spattered, tear-stained piece of paper. Sometimes pain needs to be revisited, and sometimes the victim doesn't even know why. They just know they must. Jarin now revisited his pain, reread the lyrics that pain had given birth to.

> *Whipped and beaten*
> *A son of blood and pain*
> *I raise my eyes and cry to heaven*
> *Will father ever love me again?*

Jarin felt the scars on his back throb in remembrance. Black hatred rose in him like dark waters in a deep well. He wondered if his father knew how much he hated him, how hot his rage burned. It wasn't about the music, despite what his dad might think—it was about love. Or rather, the absence of love. Jarin's desire for love was so intense that his father's refusal to give it spawned this terrible hatred. Whoever said that love and hate are twins knew what they were talking about.

He could recall his childhood with crystal clarity, could remember when his mother was still alive, when his father loved him, and the recollection of happy times now lost spawned bitterness that overshadowed the memories of joy. Sometimes he thought it would have been better if he had been born into an abusive family because then he wouldn't know how bad things had become. A man born blind doesn't miss his sight as much as a man who loses his sight halfway through life.

He knew exactly when his father had stopped loving him. It had been, and still was, the darkest day of his life.

The day of the dare.

"What are you, scared?"

"No," Jarin replied. "It's just dumb, that's all."

"Come on," Marcus retorted. "What can go wrong? If you can't make it, you just jump in the river."

Dave said nothing. He was the follower of their tiny group. Whatever Marcus and Jarin agreed on was okay with him. If they decided to jump off the edge of the Grand Canyon without parachutes, he would blindly follow like a lemming leaping to its death. Not that he was retarded or anything, but...well, his mental motor was closer to a four-cylinder than a V-8.

"What's the point?" Jarin said. "I mean, what are we trying to prove?"

"We're not trying to prove anything," Marcus replied. "It's just a dare, plain and simple."

"It's stupid."

"Whatever. You in or not?"

"Not."

Marcus slung an arm around his best bud's shoulder. A sly grin curled across his face, reminding Jarin of the Cheshire Cat. "Listen, Jarin, you know that new girl at school? Poppy Zelcar?"

"Yeah," Jarin said cautiously. He'd been smitten with Poppy Zelcar since he'd first seen her. Her beauty, combined with her strange, wonderful name that rolled off the tongue like melted butter, had sent his heart racing. His dreams of her had not been rated PG.

"Well," Marcus said, still grinning, "I happen to know she has the hots for you."

"Are you serious?"

"As a dead baby." Marcus had a knack for gruesome metaphors. "Now, imagine if poor Poppy found out that the man of her dreams had chickened out of a harmless little dare."

"You wouldn't."

"Maybe, maybe not. Can you afford to take that chance?"

Jarin was silent, weighing the risk versus the possible reward. Poppy's supple curves and lovely heart-shaped face danced through his mind as Dave stood nearby, smiling vacantly like a numbskull.

"Still not sure?" Marcus piped up. "Let me help you along. Just imagine your precious Poppy in the arms of some jock on the football team. Imagine his tongue down her throat, his hands up her—"

"Okay! Okay! Shut up already. I'm in."

"Cool. Let's do it. The train will be here in less than ten minutes."

They trotted down the tracks that ran past Jarin's house, being careful where they placed their feet. The distance between the ties was shorter than the length of their stride, so their gait was rather awkward. Once, Jarin mistimed his step, and his foot slipped on the loose gravel between the ties. He nearly went down, but after a few staggering steps, he regained his balance.

Marcus grinned at him. "Easy there, clumsy."

"Blow me."

"I want a meal, not a snack."

"I'll snack ya, asshole."

"Poppy's going to be very disappointed when she finds out you like boys."

"Fuck you."

"I rest my case."

It was the familiar banter of boyhood friends, and it passed the time until they came to the train trestle that spanned the Hudson River. The river was roughly three hundred yards wide at this point, and it was about a seventy-five-foot drop from the trestle to the water.

Jarin took a few steps out onto the bridge. There was nothing but empty space between the ties and he could look down and see the Hudson below. The water had an orange film on it, pollution from the factory two miles upriver. "This is a bad idea," he muttered.

Marcus replied, "Got one word for you—Poppy."

"This is blackmail."

"Hey, what are friends for?"

They headed for the middle of the trestle, careful where they put their feet. The gaps between the ties weren't wide enough for someone to fall through, but a foot could easily get caught between them, resulting in a twisted or broken ankle.

From behind them came the long, drawn-out blast of an air-horn, followed by the ding-ding-ding of the barriers coming down at the railroad crossing by Jarin's house. The trestle began to shake.

"Hurry up!" Marcus urged. "It's coming!"

"Relax," Jarin said, wishing he could take his own advice. "We're in the middle, for crying out loud."

"Remember the dare. Soon as the train hits the trestle, we start running for the other side, see if we can beat it there."

"Just remember to jump into the river if you can't make it."

"No shit, Sherlock."

"Got it, Davey?"

Dave nodded, his trademark blank grin etched on his face.

"All right," Marcus yelled. "Here it comes!"

The freight engine rounded the bend, chugging along at a good clip. For some reason, Jarin was reminded of a huge snake bearing down on them. The engineer must have seen them, for he gave a long blast with the horn. The trestle began to rock and sway.

"Go! Go! Go!" Marcus shouted, turning to run as the train sped out onto the bridge. "Last one there is crushed meat!"

The thought of being ground to pulp under the train's thundering wheels spurred Jarin into motion. He began to run for the other side of the trestle, taking the ties two at a time. The river flashed by below him. His entire body thrummed with the vibration of the approaching freight engine.

"Come on!" Marcus, comfortably in the lead, yelled over his shoulder.

Dave's mouth hung open in a dumb grin. He looked like a drooling idiot trying to catch flies, arms pumping mechanically. But even he was outrunning Jarin...

...who glanced back and saw the train a mere thirty yards behind him. Shit. It was at least fifty yards to the other side of the trestle. Looked like he was going for a swim.

But as he prepared to turn that thought into action...

...his foot slipped between two ties.

He lurched forward and heard a loud SNAP! Sharp pain flared in his ankle. Momentum threw his body over the side of the trestle, but his foot refused to come free. He screamed "NOOOOOOOOO!!!"

...and then the train...

Jarin shuddered as the phantom pain pulsed through his stumps. He reached down and massaged the hard nubs of flesh and bone. The iron wheels of the train had acted like giant razors, shearing off both legs at mid-thigh. A stupid dare, all for the sake of a girl, had damned him to a wheelchair for the rest of his life. But at least Poppy had visited him in the hospital.

"Jarin? You awake?"

"Hi, Poppy. Yeah, I'm awake. Come on in."

"How are you doing?" She looked distinctly uncomfortable.

"I'm okay," he said, then waved toward the chair next to his bed. "Have a seat."

"I can't stay long, Jarin. Besides, I'm not sure what to say."

"Say whatever you would normally say. I'm the same person."

"No, Jarin, you're not."

Shock ran through him like an electrical current. Was she being unusually honest or unnecessarily cruel? "Of course I am," he protested. "I'm still the same ol' Jarin."

"I'm sorry, Jarin, but you're not. You're different now. You have to face that."

"Face what?"

"That things have changed."

"What do you mean? What things?"

"Well...us, for one."

"What are you trying to say?" He knew exactly what she was trying to say but wanted to make her say it.

"I...I can't be with you, Jarin. I just can't do it."

"Why not? You mean to tell me the only reason you liked me was because I had legs?"

"That's not..." She sighed. "Look, don't make this harder than it has to be. If it makes it any easier, I've met someone else. Matter of fact, he's the one who drove me here to see you."

"Let me guess—some jock, right?"

She blinked in surprise. "How did you know?"

He turned his head so she wouldn't see him weep. "Go away," he whispered. "Just go the hell away."

"Jarin, I'm sor—"

"GET OUT OF HERE!"

She hesitated another moment. He wanted to look at her but was afraid he would see that there were no tears in her eyes. "Goodbye," she said after a few seconds of silence. "I'll be seeing you."

But that had been a lie. He'd never seen her again, save for the occasional class they had together. Even now, two years after the accident, it still hurt to see her with her jock boyfriend, to imagine the two of them down on Lover's Lane, fogging up the windows. That

13

should have been him. But he couldn't blame her. No girl wanted a guy without legs, not even if he lost them trying to win her. Man, life was so screwed up sometimes. *If God really pulls the strings, then He must have a cruel streak in Him,* Jarin thought. *He took my legs, took my girl, and then to top it all off, He took my father's love away from me.*

He could have survived his dad's betrayal if his mother had been around to give him strength. But when Dad started beating him, he also started beating her, and it didn't take her long to reach the end of her rope—literally. In a drunken stupor, she hung herself.

Jarin added to his song the night of her funeral.

> *Nooses and gravestones*
> *I weep for mother gone*
> *Oh, dear God in Heaven, tell me*
> *Why'd she leave her loveless son?*

Now, years later, tears streamed down his face as he stared at the monitor and reread those words. *Why did you have to go, Mom? Why did you have to leave me? If I could endure his rage, why couldn't you? You told me time and time again about God and how much you trust Him, then you went and denied that trust with your actions. You trusted in a noose rather than in God.*

Trust, Jarin mused. Such a small thing, but without it...without it you have nothing. And when trust is broken...well, whoever said that time heals all wounds lied through their teeth. Some wounds just never mend.

"We'd really like to take you with us, Jarin, but..." Marcus shrugged helplessly.

Jarin refused to let him off the hook that easy. "But what?"

Marcus fidgeted, unable to meet Jarin's eyes. "Uh, don't take this wrong, man, but...well, you know, it's kind of a pain dragging you in and out of the car. I mean, if we had a van with a lift, that'd be different, but..."

Shame mixed with bitter anger rose like bile to burn his throat. His words were tight, clipped, razor-edged as he rasped, "Sorry my hanging out with you is such a hassle. I'll try to forget we were ever friends."

"That's not what I meant, Jarin."

"I know what you meant, Marcus, and you can go to hell."

"Jarin, try to understand what it's like. It really is a pain."

Jarin looked his best friend dead in the eye. "Pain, Marcus? You want to talk about pain? I'll never walk again because you talked me into some stupid dare. I'll spend the rest of my life in this frigging wheelchair, and it's your fault. So don't lecture me about pain—I'm a fucking expert on the subject."

"Listen, if you really want to come with us, I think I can—"

"Forget it. I'd rather be alone than spend time with scumbags like you. Just get away from me, you traitorous little prick."

"Okay, man, I'm going. Be seeing you."

"No, you won't."

"Really, man, I'll be around. Trust me."

"I did, Marcus. I did. But never again."

Yeah, his old friends sucked, and he never bothered to make new ones. Once bitten, twice shy, as the saying went. Then again, they also said when you got bucked off a horse, you should climb right back on. But screw that, he'd stick with the first saying. He still felt poisoned by betrayal's bite.

But at least he still had his music.

He picked up the remote control to his stereo and punched the power button. The room hummed with electricity for a moment, then a blast of hard rock exploded from the speakers—the same ones his father had demolished. He'd managed to repair them. The walls shook to the thunderous sounds of Bon Jovi singing about living on a prayer.

He picked up his guitar—a new one because hadn't been able to fix the one his dad smashed—and began to play the familiar tune. The music and his guitar, the only things that would never betray him. The only things he could trust until the world turned to ash.

"Hey!" His father pounded on the door. "Turn that crap down!"

Jarin almost obeyed, as he had ever since that brutal beating not so long ago, but then he realized he couldn't. What would come next would be painful, but he needed it to finish his song.

"You hear me, Jarin? Believe me, boy, you don't want me to come in there."

No, I don't. But yes, I do. His fingers blitzed across the strings. The screech of electrified thunder sizzled through the room.

"All right, you asked for it." Gary kicked the door open so hard the knob left a hole in the wall. The red motes in his eyes swirled like crazed banshees. He shoved a finger in Jarin's face, so close that Jarin could see the dirt under his nail. "Last chance, boy. Turn it down, or I'll ram that stereo right up your worthless ass."

"Take your best shot, Dad, because this is the last time you'll ever lay a hand on me."

"You threatening me, son?" The red specks compressed together like angry storm clouds. "I thought you'd learned your lesson last time, but I guess I was wrong. Round two coming right up." His hand whipped around.

The blow rocked Jarin's head. He shook it to clear away the fog, then smiled up at his father. "That the best you got?"

With a roar, his dad started swinging...

...and Jarin's world dissolved into a dark place full of blood and pain. He felt his eyes swell shut. Felt his flesh torn open by the wedding band his dad never bothered to remove after his mom's death. Felt the crackle of cartilage as his nose shattered. Felt his lips crushed against his teeth. Felt the blood running hot and thick down the back of his throat, choking him.

Yet through it all he never stopped smiling.

At last, his father stopped, sweating dripping from his face, chest heaving from exertion. His knuckles were raw and bloody. "That should teach you," he growled between gasps. "Whatta ya got to say now, huh, boy?"

Jarin reached up and wiped the blood from his eyes. He looked down, realizing he had clung to the guitar through the entire beating. Blood dripped from the strings like crimson tears. He looked back up at his dad. "Thank you," he whispered. "I think I can finish my song now."

———

Hours later, Jarin listened to the *chiiiiirrreep-chiiiiirrreeep* of crickets in the nearby marsh mingling with the deep bass croak of the bullfrogs. *Nature's music,* he thought, taking a deep breath and smelling the night air. Fireflies winked at him from the thick brush along the edge of the train tracks.

It had taken a long time and hard work to maneuver his wheelchair out of the house, down the road, and onto the tracks, but he'd managed. Now he just sat, listening to the dark, gazing up at the stars that twinkled like the eyes of a thousand angels. Behind him, just around the bend, was the trestle that had taken his legs. He felt bitterness wanting to come, but he refused to let it. Not tonight. Not any night ever again.

He looked down at the paper in his hand, breath wheezing wetly through his broken nose. *It's done,* he thought, reading the words he'd written just a few hours ago, using a simple pencil dipped in his own blood, the blood his father had beaten out of him. *My song is finished.*

A train whistled in the distance.

He let the paper fall from his hands. The breeze whisked it up and carried it into the brush where it impaled itself on the thorns of a locust tree. For some reason it reminded Jarin of the sign that hung over Christ's head on the cross.

The train sounded again, the ghostly echo of its horn floating through the night, riding the wisps of fog rising from the marsh.

It was time.

Jarin threw back his head and yelled,

"DAAAAAAAAAADDDDDD!!!!" He repeated the call again and again until his lungs ached.

Then he waited, watching his house, just up the road.

A light came on, the yellow glow spilling into the dark. A door slammed shut. A few minutes later, Jarin heard the gravel crunching under his father's feet as he approached. Though he couldn't see them, Jarin imagined the angry red motes in his dad's eyes.

"Hello, Dad."

"What the *hell* is going on? What are you doing out here at four o'clock in the friggin' morning?" Gary's old flannel robe flapped around his pale, knobby knees.

"Finishing my song."

"I've had enough of your games, boy. Get back to the house, or I'll make the pounding I gave you earlier seem like a make-out session with that Poppy slut you got the hots for."

"Okay," Jarin said quietly as the train horn blew a third time. *And the cock crowed thrice,* he thought for some crazy reason. Maybe he was going insane. Not that it mattered much anymore. "I need some help. My wheels are stuck between the ties."

"Are you fucking kidding me?" Gary swore. But he came over and reached for the wheelchair.

It took Jarin less than two seconds to snag his dad's wrist in the stainless-steel handcuffs. The other cuff went around his own wrist, chaining them together.

"What the—" Gary jerked his hand back. The bracelet bit into his wrist, holding him fast. "Let me go right now, you little piece of shit, or I'll—"

"You'll what?" Jarin interrupted with a smile. "Face it, Dad, you've just run out of luck."

As if on cue, the train rounded the bend, its head-light carving through the night like a luminescent blade.

Gary tore frantically at the cuffs. His nails slid right off the polished metal. "Let me go!" he screamed. "Are you crazy? That train will be here in less than thirty seconds!"

"I know." Jarin was still smiling. "But I have nothing left to live for."

"Let me go!"

"Say you love me, Dad."

"Do you hear me? LET ME GO!"

"Tell me you love me."

"I'll fucking kill you!"

The train roared closer. The crossing barriers dropped into place.

"We have about ten seconds left, Dad. Tell me you love me. Give me a reason to live." Jarin was still smiling, but now there were tears in his eyes as well.

"Never," Gary hissed. "You hear me, you little bastard? I never loved you! Never!"

Five seconds...

"I know," Jarin said, all the pain in the world compressed into those two words, tears running down his cheeks like dew off rose petals.

Four seconds...

"Jarin! For God's sake, let me go!"

Three seconds...

"Love me."

Two seconds...

"Okay! All right! I love you! I love you, Jarin!"

One second...

"You're too late, Dad." One last tear fell from Jarin's eye...

...as the train filled the night...

...and then, like Jarin's song, it was over.

———

"Yo, Sarge." Blue and red lights flashed off the cop's badge.

"Yeah?"

"I found something on this thorn tree over here."

"What is it?"

"A poem or song or something, written in blood."

"Read it to me."

"*I could have lived without the music / I never needed my guitar / All I wanted was Daddy's love / But all he gave me were these scars.*"

"That's it?"

"That's all, Sarge. It's signed Jarin Harper."

"Love sure is a bitch, isn't it?"

"You can say that again."

NAÏVETÉ

The voices of despair call him to the razor's dance
A suicidal tango to a red-veined rhythm
A sodden symphony summoning him
to the salvation of Jack Daniels

An altar, a vow, a good noose around his finger
A child's innocence chaining him to the emptiness
Love gone cold and sweetheart dreams
broken upon adulterous rocks

Drunken prayers to a bottled idol and has God damned him
for worshipping at a bourbon altar?
He eats the deafened bread yet hungers still
and redemption cannot be found in crimson wine

Sin for sin, the carnal vengeance of adulterous screams
serves only to mock his desperate cries
In the heat of illicit salvation is found only a cross of guilt
and the razor's song

Glistening tears reflect hopelessness honed
His red-rimmed eyes gaze into hell's dark promise
Then an innocent voice, "Daddy, can I shave too?"
and the angel's plea hushes the bloodthirsty blade

PREY

AUTHOR'S NOTE

One day while hunting, I watched a hawk snag a chipmunk and proceed to devour the critter while it was still alive, tearing strips of meat from its squirming body. In that moment, this story sparked to life. And yeah, once again, the theme of abusive relationships rears its ugly head.

"What's that?" Nine-year-old Tammy Preston pointed at the circling speck way up in the clear blue sky. A mild breeze ruffled her red hair, blowing a few stray strands across her heavily freckled face.

Her brother John, a twelve-year-old who looked more like sixteen, his five-foot-seven-inch frame packed with hard muscle due to his constant weightlifting, studied her chubby finger for a moment. *How did she get so fat?* Dumb question really because he already knew the answer. Tammy had coped with Dad's abuse by stuffing herself with any available junk food. Chocolate chip cookies happened to be her favorite.

He remembered one time about two years ago when they sat on the sofa watching *The Lion King,* two boxes of cookies between them. One for him, one for her. The TV blared but not loudly enough to drown out the wicked sound of flesh smacking flesh in the master bedroom as Dad beat the crap out of Mom. The beating stopped just before the movie ended, but by then Tammy had eaten *both* boxes of cookies. John had turned the TV off for a moment but couldn't stand to hear his mother crying, so he had quickly turned it back on. He felt guilty as he watched a *Knight Rider* rerun, but if he tried to go to Mom, then Dad would slap him around too.

Tammy had gone into the kitchen and returned with a handful of Twinkies. She promptly began shoveling the yellow sponge cakes down her gullet, eyes fixed on the crime-fighting antics of Michael Knight and his talking car. John watched her stuff herself and knew she was praying. *Please, God, don't let him come in here. Don't let him beat us tonight too. Please, God, don't let Daddy hurt me. Please make him leave us alone.* He knew her thoughts because they were his thoughts as well. Thankfully, on that particular night, God happened to be listening. Usually He wasn't, though, and for John, the only thing worse than listening to Dad beat up Mom was listening to him beat up on his little sister.

But he didn't have to worry about that anymore. The thought comforted him, and he smiled.

Tammy saw the grin. "What're you so happy about?"

"Nothing. Now, what did you ask me?"

She pointed at the speck in the sky again. "Can you tell what that is?"

He lifted the binoculars hanging from a strap around his neck and gazed up at the bird riding the thermals above them. "Red-tailed hawk," he said, lowering the glasses.

"What's it doin'?"

"Flying."

"No duh, Johnny."

"Okay, it's hunting. And don't call me Johnny. I hate that."

"You call me Fats sometimes."

"That's different. It's a pet name. It shows affection."

"So why can't Johnny be a pet name?"

"Because it's a little boy's name. I'm almost a teenager."

"Whatever."

"You want to find some more birds? Or do you want to stand here and bicker the rest of the afternoon?"

"There aren't any birds here," she said. "These woods are too small."

The wood lot between their house and the main road only covered an acre, but John knew Tammy was mistaken. "There are birds in here, but they won't come out until you're quiet." He raised the binoculars again and scanned the trees.

Tammy plopped down on a mossy stump and scratched a mosquito bite on her knee as she looked around. "John, look, I see something."

"Where?"

She pointed at a brush thicket about twenty-five yards away. "See it?"

He aimed the binoculars at the object and fiddled with the focus. "It's a bird's nest."

"Really? What kind?"

John panned left until he found what he was looking for—the owner of the nest. The bird's sandy-gray color helped it blend into the bushes, but once you knew where to look, the bird's white tail-trim and dark spots stood out. "It's a mourning dove," he said.

"Why do they call it a morning dove? Does it only come out in the morning?"

"Not a 'morning' dove. A *mourning* dove." He spelled it out for her. "M-O-U-R-N-I-N-G. They call it that because it always sounds sad. You've seen them at Mom's feeder before. They sound like this." He pursed his lips and mimicked the dove call. *Coo-ah, coo-coo-coo.*

Tammy shrugged. She didn't pay much attention to the bird feeder Mom loved so much.

"Mourning doves mate for life," John explained, hoping she wouldn't ask what "mate" meant. "So, if that's the female by the nest, the male must be nearby."

A shadow darkened the ground right in front of them. They both looked up to see that the hawk had dropped lower in the sky. Tammy suddenly spotted the other dove sitting in the top of a tall dead tree. "Johnny!" she exclaimed. "There's the daddy dove."

"Where?"

She pointed...

...as the hawk dove from the sky like a bullet.

"No!" John yelled, realizing what was about to happen. He knew he should cover Tammy's eyes, but he felt hypnotized by the savage drama unfolding high above him.

The hawk slammed into the dove at 90 mph, blowing him right off the branch. Feathers exploded into the air. The dove cried out in terror as the hawk bore him down to the ground, then flailed helplessly as the hawk's vicious beak ripped raw strips of meat from his body. John was caught between horror and fascination. *My God, he's being eaten alive.*

The female dove heard the cries of the male and flew from the brush, attacking the hawk's head, desperately beating it with her wings, trying to make it let go of her mate.

"What's she doing?" Tammy cried. "She'll be killed too!"

Her words proved prophetic. The hawk's bloody beak lashed out and caught the dove in midair, tearing out her throat with one quick rip. She fell to the dirt, wings flapping feebly as the life bled out of her.

"NOOOOOOO..." Tammy screamed, tears running down her face. "Leave her alone!"

"It's too late," John said as the hawk continued to devour the male dove. He was surprised the red tail showed little fear of them. It merely kept a wary eye on them as it gobbled down its meal. *Maybe it was someone's pet once. Maybe that's why it's not afraid of people.*

Tammy sobbed quietly until the hawk finished its meal. Then, with one last baleful glance in their direction, the red tail took off. Its large wings carried it above the trees and up into the sky.

Tammy watched it go and muttered, "Fuckin' bird."

The profanity shocked John. "Hey, where'd you learn that word?"

"I'm nine years old, John. I know about bad words."

"Mom ever hears you saying that, she'll ground you for a month."

"I don't care. I hate that hawk."

"Still shouldn't use that word."

"What are you, my *father*?"

That stung. More than John cared to admit. Not wanting to face the hurt, he went over to the nest in the thicket, careful not to look at the mangled birds on the ground. He had enough bad memories to keep him up at night without adding to them. He reached into the bush and pulled out the nest cupping one hand underneath to keep it from falling apart. "Hey, Tam," he said. "C'mere."

"But the doves..."

"Just don't look at them. Now come here. I want to show you something."

She came reluctantly, giving the carcasses a wide berth, then deliberately turned her back to them as she faced John. "What?"

He held the nest down low so she could see into it.

Her eyes lit up like Christmas lights. "Oh!"

The baby dove regarded them with trusting eyes, too young to know it was supposed to be afraid, and made small peeping noises.

"It's hungry," Tammy said. "But..." She looked over her shoulder, then quickly snapped her head back around, having just glimpsed the gory mess that had been the chick's father.

"But its parents are dead," John finished for her.

"We can't just leave it here. The hawk might come back."

A baby dove, John thought. *Nice snack for a hawk.* But

he didn't say anything so morbid to Tammy. He didn't need her to start bawling again. Instead, he said, "Let's take it home and see if we can find it some food."

"Yay! Do you think Mom will let us keep it?"

"Let's go find out."

———

Pamela Preston stared out the sliding glass doors at the young elm tree with a double-tiered bird feeder mounted on a pole beside it. The feeder thrived on sunny afternoons like this, and she just sat and watched her feathered friends. Mourning doves strutted gracefully through the lush grass under the elm, picking at the seeds the other birds tossed to the ground. Chickadees splashed in the nearby birdbath, their trilling little *chee-chee-chee* bringing a smile to her lips. It felt good to smile, for there hadn't been much to smile about during her ten years of marriage to Harold. But those days were behind her now.

A blue jay perched atop the feeder as if it was a throne and he was the monarch of this bird kingdom while a pair of cardinals—both male, Pamela knew by their bright red color—bickered over pecking order.

John and Tammy didn't understand her fascination with birds, but that was okay. They had each coped with Harold's abuse in their own way. Tammy found solace in sweets, Pam found it bird watching, and John immersed himself in weightlifting. This, combined with a growth spurt, made him look sixteen instead of twelve, his muscles bigger than many high school seniors. Those muscles came in handy when defending his little sister against any bully who dared called her

Fats or Fatso. He reserved those names for himself, and though an outsider might think it cruel when he called Tammy those names, Pam knew it was just his clumsy way of showing brotherly affection.

The birds suddenly scattered into the air in a flurry of wings, jolting her back to the here and now. Only the kingly blue jay stuck around. He perched at the top of the elm and screamed at the invader who had sent his loyal subjects scurrying. The shiny black grackle, now squatting atop the feeder where the jay had been before, cocked its head at the dethroned king and screamed back defiantly. *Grawk! Grawk!*

"Damn grackle," Pam muttered as she reached for the Winchester .22 semiautomatic rifle she kept by the door for just such an occasion. She hated grackles. They were the bullies of the bird world. Whenever they showed up, all other birds fled until they left. Pam shot them whenever she had the chance. No neighbors were within a mile, so she never had to worry about where the bullet went if she missed. Not that she missed much. It was less than ten yards from the house to the feeder, and the .22 sported a scope.

She opened the glass door just a crack and braced the gun against the frame. Jay and grackle went on waging a screaming war as she aligned the crosshairs on the grackle's head and pulled the trigger.

Ka-pop!

The dead grackle tumbled to the ground as the blue jay, unfazed by the gunshot, continued to scream at it. It took almost no time for the other birds to return. They fed and frolicked, apparently unconcerned about their dead relative, maybe even glad he was gone.

Pam stayed locked to the scope, studying the

grackle. Bright red blood leaked from the small hole in the bird's head and dappled the black feathers. But as time ticked by, it was not the grackle that Pam saw, but her husband Harold. Her mind tricked her eyes, convinced her that she had just shot the man who beat her half to death for ten long years before she found the guts to bundle up her children and run away in the middle of a January blizzard. She saw the blood on the bird and imagined the .22 bullet buried deep in Harold's diseased brain. It had to be diseased—no normal mind could conjure up the things he had done to her. Mere beatings she could have endured, but the other things...the evil, twisted things he made her suffer...she'd been unable to endure those.

Dear God, she prayed as she continued to look through the scope. *Where were You all those years? Couldn't You hear my cries? How many times does a wife have to have the shit beat out of her before You listen? How many times does she have to be raped by beer bottles before You decide to do something? How much pain is enough?*

The final straw came Christmas night two years ago. Harold's gift to her was a sixteen-ounce Budweiser bottle used as a phallus. But he rammed too hard, and the bottle broke. The pain felt like a red-hot razor cutting her in two, but it cleared her mind and made her realize she had to leave him before he killed her or the kids.

She blinked, and the image of her husband lying dead beneath the bird feeder faded from her mind. She was surprised to find tears on her face, the memories she had just relived still too fresh to be faced without pain.

Tammy and John came around the corner of the

house, and she quickly brushed away the tears, not wanting them to see her cry. She put the gun back in its place and pasted a smile on her lips as they bounded up the patio steps, John carefully balancing a nest in his hands. A tiny head peeked up over the edge, and Pam instantly identified the chick as a mourning dove.

"Hi, Mom," John greeted as Tammy opened the glass door. "Look what we found."

"John, I've told you about handling baby birds. Now the chick has your smell on it, and the parents won't—"

"Its parents are dead," John interrupted. "Hawk got 'em."

"Can we keep it, Mom?" Tammy pleaded. "Can we? It doesn't got a home."

"Doesn't *have* a home," Pam corrected automatically, one of the side effects of being an English teacher. She looked at John. "How do you know a hawk killed them?"

"We were there when it happened."

"In our woods?"

"Yup. It got the male first, then killed the female when she tried to help her mate. Happened right in front of us."

"Mommy?" Tammy's lower lip quivered. "It ate the daddy dove."

Pam looked at John again. "It ate it right there in front of you?"

"Yup. It was weird, Mom. That hawk wasn't scared of us at all."

"That *is* strange."

"So can we keep the dove?"

"I don't know..."

Just then the chick began peeping, its fuzzy little

head bobbing this way and that with the clumsy lack of coordination of the young and innocent.

Pam made up her mind. "John, get some of the left-over corn from the fridge."

"Yay!" Tammy yelled, startling the dove. "We're gonna keep it!"

"Are you going to give it a name?"

"Already did." John grinned. "Tammy named it while we were carrying it back here."

"What is it?"

"Fuzzy."

"Fuzzy?"

"Yup."

Pam looked at her daughter. "You know it won't always be fuzzy like this, honey."

"So? It's fuzzy now, so I want to name it Fuzzy."

John warmed the corn in the microwave and brought it over.

"Mush it up," said Pam. "He's too young to eat whole kernels."

"What's it usually eat?" asked Tammy.

"Regurgitated food."

"What's that?"

"It means its mom and dad would throw up, and Fuzzy would eat the puke," John explained, relishing the chance to revolt her.

"Grrooooooosss!!!"

It took some work, but they managed to get some of the corn mush down Fuzzy's throat. Soon the little dove fell sound asleep, tummy full.

"Can it stay in my room?" Tammy asked.

"Sure, sweetie."

Tammy gingerly picked up the nest, not wanting to

awaken Fuzzy. She paused halfway to her room and turned to ask, "Do ya think Fuzzy would like part of a Twinkie?"

Pam smiled. "No, hon. Twinkies aren't good for birds."

"Okay. Guess I'll just have to eat the whole thing myself." Tammy disappeared into her room with her new friend.

———

Late that night, Pam reread the note she had received in the mail today, the one she didn't dare tell Tammy or John about. No return address, and its message was simple, blunt, and terrifying.

Pamela (a.k.a. Traitorous Bitch),

Just wanted to let you know I'm coming for ya. Don't bother trying to run again, Pam—I'll be watching the house. You won't get away so easily this time. Gotta say, you gave me one hell of a chase. What's it been, a year since you ran off with the kiddies? You didn't really think you could get away from me forever, did ya, Pammy? I hope not.

By the way, got a little present for you. Did you know Budweiser comes in twenty-five-ounce bottles? Trust me, you're gonna love it. I might even let Tammy in on the fun. 'Bout time she learned what it takes to please a man.

No signature, but there was no need for one. He'd made it perfectly clear who the letter was from. Fear struck her heart.

I'll be watching the house...

She stared out the window at the dark, wondering if he watched her from the shadows. She suddenly remembered she had undressed without bothering to shut the blinds. Had he stared at her naked body and imagined violating it with a beer bottle?

Got a little present for you...you're gonna love it...

Goosebumps shuddered across her skin as she hurried over to draw the blinds.
And that evil chuckle that she heard?
Had to be her imagination.
Right?

———

The next morning, John woke before anyone else and took his bowl of Cheerios out onto the patio to enjoy the cool morning air. Dew glistened on the grass, which really needed to be mowed. Maybe he would do that later today. Unbeknownst to him, had he gone around to the other side of the house, he would have seen the ground under his bedroom window had no dew on it. He also would have seen a set of footprints in the grass, leading away from the house and into the nearby woods.

The sliding glass doors opened, and Tammy came out, cradling Fuzzy in one hand and a Twinkie in the other. White cream filling speckled the corners of her mouth, and yellow crumbs dribbled down the front of her pajamas. She plopped herself down on the step beside John.

"Morning, Fats," he greeted.

"Don't call me Fats," she replied automatically.

John reached over and rubbed Fuzzy's head. "How's Fuzz doing this morning?"

As if in reply, the little dove let loose a loud peep.

"Yeah, I'll bet you miss your mom."

"I'm its mom now," said Tammy.

A shadow slid across the step right below them.

John looked up. "It's the hawk."

"Should I take Fuzzy inside?"

"Nah. That hawk won't do nothing long as we're here."

Tammy glared up at the red tail. "I hate you, you ugly bird."

The hawk screamed back, its piercing cry tearing through the crisp morning air.

"Something spooky about that bird," John muttered. "It's like he's got a hard-on for us or something."

Tammy promptly asked, "What's a hard-on?"

John blushed. "Uh, never mind. It's just that the hawk acts like it's mad at us or something."

"Maybe it just doesn't like people."

"Maybe."

Fuzzy chose that moment to hop out of Tammy's hand. He landed on his feet but promptly lost his balance and tumbled down the patio steps. He landed on the dewy grass and shook his tiny head bewilderedly as if to say, *Wow, what just happened?*

John tried not to laugh, but the little dove had

looked pretty funny bumbling down the steps like a fuzzy rubber ball.

"Don't laugh at him. He could have been hurt." Tammy went down the steps and picked him up. "Oh, Fuzzy," she cooed. "Are you okay?"

John saw the shadow a second too late. "Tammy! Look out!"

The hawk plucked Fuzzy right out of her hand without so much as scratching her. But its powerful wings swept across her face and bowled her over as she screamed in horror.

The impact of its wings against Tammy's face unbalanced the red tail, forcing it to release its prey or else crash into the ground. Fuzzy, peeping in terror, fell back into the dewy grass as the hawk rose back into the sky, screaming in frustrated rage.

John ran over, scooped up Fuzzy, and checked him over. He found one tiny nick on the bird's back, nothing more. "You're one lucky bird, Fuzz."

Pam came flying out of the house, eyes full of sleep grit. "What's wrong? What happened? Are you guys all right?"

"The haaawwwwwk..." Tammy sobbed, more scared than hurt.

"What about the hawk? John, tell me what happened!"

"The hawk grabbed Fuzzy right out of her hand. Its wings hit her in the face and knocked her down. She's okay, just scared."

"The hawk took Fuzz right out of her *hand*?"

"Yup. Told you this hawk ain't normal."

"*Isn't* normal." Pam kneeled in front of Tammy and brushed away her tears. "You all right, honey?"

Sniffling, Tammy nodded.

John handed Fuzzy over to her. "Here ya go, Fats."

"Don't call me Fats."

Pam smiled at the familiar exchange. "I guess you'll have to be careful when you bring Fuzzy outside. I think the hawk wants him even more than you do."

"Then the hawk can kiss my ass."

John doubled over in laughter.

"Tammy!" Pam scolded. "Where did you hear that kind of language?"

"School."

"If I hear you talk like that again, you'll be grounded. Understand?"

"But Mom—"

"Don't you 'but Mom' me. Trashy people talk trashy. You want to be trash?"

"No."

"Good." Pam ruffled her daughter's hair. "Now be careful out here. I'm going back to bed."

High overhead, the hawk let out another scream.

———

Three weeks later, Pam's nerves were like frayed rubber bands stretched to the max, just waiting to snap. *How long is he going to do this to us? How long is he just going to watch? God, I can't take this much longer.*

She hardly slept anymore, feeling his eyes watching her in the dark. She heard his footsteps in every creak of the house, his breath in every whisper of the wind. She kept thinking she heard his evil chuckle, his vile laugh, a sound that sent knives straight to her heart. It was the soundtrack to her nightmares, her time in hell, and even the memory of that laugh scraped her soul raw.

She considered running again, further this time, maybe even to another country. But she knew it was useless. He had found her, and now there was no escape. She realized she had been stupid to keep her name the same. She'd been a fool, clinging to some worthless part of her former life, using her name as an anchor to her past while she fled into the future. But now that anchor had dragged the unwelcome part of her past into the present. It was like thinking you had hooked a trophy fish only to discover you had only snagged a smelly old boot. Except this "boot" could kill her. *Wanted* to kill her.

And probably would.

———

The next day was Saturday. John and Tammy rose shortly after dawn to have a bowl of cereal on the patio together. It had become a weekend ritual for them, sitting side by side on the top step, facing east so the rising sun could caress their faces with gentle fingers of warm light. The heat sometimes made them drowsy, but they didn't dare fall asleep, not even for a few moments. The hawk was never far away, and in the last three weeks, Fuzzy had grown into a healthy young bird, a tasty meal for any raptor.

"How long before he can fly, ya think?" Tammy asked, putting aside her empty cereal bowl. A milk mustache ran across her upper lip.

"Not sure," said John. "He's been flapping his

wings, getting stronger. Won't be long now. Few days, maybe a week."

"Will he leave us?"

"Maybe. He's a wild animal, not a pet."

"But why would he leave? We aren't bad parents. We aren't like Daddy."

"Who the fuck says I'm a bad parent, huh?" Harold Preston came around the corner of the house.

Shock nailed John's feet to the porch.

Tammy's eyes went wide as saucers. "D-d-d-dad?"

"Yuh-yuh-yuh-yes, F-F-F-Fatso?"

John slowly stood up. Already his initial shock at seeing his father was fading, replaced by fear and... something else. Something he wouldn't recognize until later as hatred. "Don't call her Fatso."

"Why not? You looked at her lately, Johnny boy? She looks like a hog ripe for the slaughterhouse."

"Just leave us alone."

"Don't gimme no lip, boy. Why don't you come over here and give ol' dad a hug?"

"I'd rather die."

Harold Preston's eyes narrowed. "You don't start minding me, son, that's exactly what's going to happen to you."

"You don't scare me."

His father threw back his head and laughed. "Of course I do, boy. This whole fucking family is scared of me. I'm like the mean ol' giant in that Jackoff and the Beanstalk story."

"Just remember that the giant dies in the end."

"Watch your mouth, sonny boy, or I'll fill it with something you won't like."

John had forgotten just how wicked his father could

be. Any shred of hope that he had changed for the better during their separation shattered under a ten-ton sledgehammer of raw realization.

Harold Preston ambled toward them. His clothes were filthy from sleeping in the woods, prowling around the house, peering in the windows as they slept. Daddy was home, and hell had returned to the Preston house.

"Tammy," John said. "Go inside."

Fear froze Tammy to the spot. She shook as if it was a cold winter night instead of a warm May morning.

"See?" Harold's grin exposed yellow, plaque-stained teeth. "Fatso knows how to listen to her father."

"Fuck you, Dad."

The grin vanished from Harold's face. "What did you just say to me?"

"I said, fuck you, *Dad*." Tammy spat his name like it left a bad taste in her mouth.

"Why, you little—" Then he spotted the small bundle of feathers nestled in her lap. "What the hell is that?"

John edged toward the patio doors. The .22 rifle was just inside, leaning against the wall. "It's a dove, dipshit. What's it look like?"

"Your mother let you have a wild animal for a pet? Has she gone completely insane?" He reached for the bird. "Gimme that."

"No!" Tammy slapped his hand away. "Leave Fuzzy alone!"

"I'll fuzzy ya, you little slut." Harold's hand came around in a vicious arc. The blow caught Tammy on the side of the head and sent her reeling. Fuzzy flapped his wings frantically and actually managed to rise a foot or two. Then Harold snatched him out of midair, his cruel fingers wrapping around the bird's throat.

"Mommy!!!" Tammy screamed.

"Kiss your fucking dove goodbye," Harold growled, lifting Fuzzy up to his face. He pursed his lips in an exaggerated pucker and kissed Fuzzy on the tip of his beak.

The shadow slashed across the ground like a black bullet.

The hawk's claws cleaved through Fuzzy's body and pinned the dove to Harold Preston's face. Wickedly curved talons impaled Harold's eyes like thick pins. When the hawk took off with its prey, it yanked Harold's eyes right out of their sockets like grisly grapes. "My eyes!" he screamed, staggering around with blood pouring down his cheeks. "I can't see! Oh god! I can't see!"

"Yeah!" John punched his fist into the air. "Kiss that, you piece of shit!"

"Fuuuuuzzzzy!!!" Tammy sobbed.

Ka-pop!

The bullet drilled Harold right through the chest. He fell to his knees beside the bird feeder, a ragged hole in his shirt. He made horrible gurgling noises, but no one within earshot gave a damn about his pain.

Pam lowered the rifle. "Die, you sick son of a bitch," she whispered. "Die." She felt so numb that she didn't even realize when John took the gun from her hands.

He walked down the steps to his father, who was moaning in agony. One hand clutched at the hole in his sternum, the other grasped at his mangled eyes. But he was still alert enough to know that someone now stood over him. "Who's there?" he gasped.

"I have something for you, Dad." John held the .22 low, the barrel only an inch from his father's forehead.

"That you, Johnny? Johnny...son...I don't wanna die. Please. Can you hear me, Johnny? What if I said I was sorry? Could you forgive me, Johnny?"

"Don't call me Johnny," he rasped, slamming back the trigger and ending his hell with a single bullet. He wasn't sure if he would ever tell his mom about the terrible things his father used to do to him with a beer bottle. There were some things she was better off not knowing.

A shadow passed over his face and as he looked up, the hawk screamed once, then vanished.

They never saw it again.

And they never forgot Fuzzy.

SHAFTED

AUTHOR'S NOTE

This one is my straight-up, no apologies, gore-fest. Back around 2000, a magazine whose name I have long since forgotten put out a submissions call seeking short stories chockful of blood-and-guts violence, so I sat down and wrote one. It didn't get selected, but their loss is your gain...well, as long as you like hardcore horror.

As the carbon hunting arrow impaled his guts, Alex Caruso thought of Sarah Teller, the woman for whom he was dying. Did he love her...or had it only been lust? The four-bladed, razor-edged broadhead, designed to cut right through a deer, sliced open his bowels and reduced his stomach to raw rags. Pain sledgehammered his system. He felt his will to live slipping away. Right now, death seemed a whole lot better than the living hell his life had become. He was nothing but a naked, spread-eagled scarecrow crucified—literally crucified, with railroad spikes driven through his wrists and ankles—to Chuck Teller's barn door while Chuck himself honed up on his archery skills by using Alex as a living, breathing target.

Behind him, the thing, reeking of blood, edged closer.

If Chuck knew the thing was there, he gave no indication. He just looked at Alex with hate-filled eyes set just a bit too far apart in a face of rugged, earthy good looks. His ham-sized fists dwarfed the compound bow, which could fire an arrow at a blistering three hundred feet per second. Even though Chuck stood fifteen yards away, Alex could see the dirt under his nails, the telltale sign of a man who made his living from the soil. Somewhere, a pig squealed. *Bacon on the hoof,* Alex thought. A strange thought for someone with an arrow in his innards. Maybe it was the pain. Or maybe it was the heat. People claimed it was the hottest August on record for upstate New York.

Chuck slid another arrow from the quiver and nocked it to the bowstring. His lips curled into a crazy sort of half-smile as he raised the bow and came to full draw, muscles rippling beneath the sweat-soaked flannel shirt he wore despite the sweltering heat. Alex heard the creak of the cams, the pulley system which powered the compound bow, and knew when Chuck released the string, those cams would snap forward with seventy pounds of thrust.

Thrust was what he had done to Sarah. Thrust into her again and again as she writhed beneath him like a sweat-slick eel, crying out in ecstasy as she raked her long, lacquered nails across his back, leaving behind raw-red stripes. Their affair had been going on for three months, and the sex was great. A bit kinky from time to time—the whole pain thing wasn't his usual style—but great, nonetheless. But had it been love? Good question. Whatever it was, he couldn't stop thinking about her. She was stuck in his mind every bit as much as the arrow was stuck in his guts.

HhhhhhiiiiiiiiissssssssZAPP!!!!

Thoughts of Sarah evaporated in a blaze of fresh pain as the second arrow drove in an inch from the first. Alex threw back his head as far as the barn door would allow, the tendons in his neck straining like rigid cords. He sucked air through clenched teeth, a sharp hiss of agony. Whatever fool had said a natural numbness accompanied painful death was a damn liar. It was just the opposite. Alex's senses were so intensified he experienced the pain on a molecular level. He felt his skin parting, layer by layer. He could actually hear the *snap-snap-snap* of his veins and muscle fibers as the arrow blades severed them, tearing through meat and tissue.

Chuck's thin lips widened into a crazy sickle of a smile when he heard Alex moan. "Hurts, huh?" Raised on a Texas cattle ranch before migrating east to take over his uncle's farm when he died, Chuck had never discarded the southwestern drawl. On any other man, the drawl would have sounded homey and charming. On Chuck, it just sounded chilling. "I'll tell ya somethin'," he said. "Ya got guts, Alex." He chuckled at his own macabre wit.

Despite the heat, Alex shivered. The chuckle had a disturbing edge to it, like a bright yellow sunflower that's been burned around the edges. He watched Chuck nock another arrow.

Behind him, the thing, reeking of blood, edged closer.

Alex looked down at the arrow shafts jutting from his abdomen. A little blood had seeped out around the carbon shafts and trickled down toward his groin. He didn't even want to think about the exit wounds. They would be gaping, gory holes. He wondered when he would start to feel the effects of blood loss, then decided it didn't matter because Chuck probably wouldn't let him live that long.

"Why'd ya do it?" Chuck asked. "Look at ya. Yer one of them slick-faced pretty boys, the kind all the women go hog wild over. Ya coulda had yer pick, for god's sake. Why'd ya have to take my Sarah?"

What should I tell him? The truth? No, the hell with that. The truth would just piss him off even more. Because the truth was, there had been nothing special that made him target Sarah other than raw animal magnetism. Alex zeroed in on her at the bar like an alpha wolf sniffing out a bitch in heat. What happened between them that night had been the most basic of instincts, a primal, even bestial, sating of lust. Love hadn't entered the equation. Things might be different *now*—Did he love her? Did he not love her? The questions floated through his mind like black angels on fluffy clouds of agony—but on that particular night, their first time together, all he'd wanted to do was screw her brains out.

"I'm waitin' for an answer," Chuck prodded.

Alex bit down on the nausea rising up inside him and said, "I don't have one to give you, Chuck. It...it just happened."

Chuck tilted his head to the side in a curious manner. He looked like that damn RCA dog. He seemed to be studying Alex in a new light, his eyes narrowing with abrupt revelation. "Do ya love my wife?" he asked. "Do ya love Sarah?"

"I...I don't know."

Chuck raised the bow, pulled, and fired in one smooth, continuous motion. The bowstring hummed a savage song. The arrow slit Alex's left cheek from the corner of his mouth to just below his ear before burying itself in the barn door. The flap of flesh flopped down, and Alex felt blood bubbling over his teeth. He cried out in pain. It felt like someone had stuffed his mouth full of red-hot coals.

"Don't lie to me, boy," Chuck growled. "Don't gimme that 'I don't know' crap. I asked you a question, and I want the truth."

Behind him, the thing, reeking of blood...

"I don't know what you want to hear!" Alex was embarrassed to feel tears gathering in the corners of his eyes. Odd that a man stripped naked and nailed to a barn with a bellyful of broadheads would feel ashamed of weeping, but there it was. "I banged your wife. Is that it? That what you want me to say? I balled her black and blue, and she *loved* it!"

"Of course she did." Chuck calmly nocked another arrow. "Sarah's a regular nympho sex kitten. She can't get enough of it. But that ain't what I asked ya. I asked if yer in love with her."

"And I told you I don't know."

"And I told *you*," Chuck growled, raising the bow, "not to lie to me." The arrow shot from the string.

Oh, sweet God in Heaven the pain I can't take this pain!!! The arrow pinned Alex's pain- and fear-shriveled manhood to the door, the slashing razors shredding everything into raw meat. Alex screamed, high and shrill. One of the pigs squealed in reply. Gradually, through a wall of the most mind-blowing agony he could not have begun to imagine in a year of a thousand hells, he became aware of words babbling from his mouth. *"KillmepleasejustkillmeIambeggingyoukillme..."*

Chuck grinned at him, a manic smile of triumph, the fanged grin of a predator who knows his prey is completely at his mercy.

Behind him, the thing...

Chuck dropped the bow onto the ground where it squelched into a pile of cow manure. Flies buzzed up at the disturbance, then settled back down to their dung dinner. He walked over to Alex, the human pincushion, and leaned against the barn in a Norman Rockwellian pose. But the cold, hard hate in his eyes shattered the pastoral illusion. "Tell me something, Alex," he said, his drawl light and easy, as if they were nothing more than two buddies discussing the latest theories of crop rotation. "Do ya really wanna die, or are you just pullin' my pud?"

The numbness Alex had craved a few minutes ago now wrapped him up in its anesthetic cocoon. The pain began to ebb, but it hardly mattered now. His wounds were mortal, the slow-kill kind, and he wanted this nightmare to end. He could spend his next life trying to figure out if he had loved Sarah in this life. "I'm not pulling anything," he told Chuck, trapped somewhere between numbness and breathless agony. "I want to die. I want you to kill me." The words sounded wet and slurred, probably from all the blood dribbling out of his slit-open cheek.

"Okay," Chuck said, "I will. I'll put ya out of your misery like you was a broke-dick dog, but ya gotta answer one question first."

"What?"

"My wife...did ya do her from behind? Ya know, doggy-style? Did ya treat her like a bitch?"

"What difference does it make?"

Chuck didn't say anything, but for the first time Alex glimpsed hurt behind the hate in the man's eyes. Guilt stabbed through him every bit as sharply as the arrows had. He had taken another man's wife. Love or lust, that was a moot point—she belonged to someone else. It suited Alex's interests to consider Chuck an unfeeling slob utterly incapable of emotion, but the pain in his eyes told a different story. Chuck loved his wife. It shouldn't have been a revelation, but it was, and Alex found it staggering.

He looked Chuck square in the eyes and said, "I want you to know, Chuck, that I'm sorry. If I could take it back..."

Chuck blinked, and just like that the pain evaporated, leaving behind only rage. "Stick yer sorry where the sun don't shine, Alex. All I want ya to do is answer my question."

"Like I said, what does it matter?"

"Just curious, is all. She never wanted to do it that way with me."

Behind him...

"I do now," the thing that had once been Sarah Teller whispered through a well of blood that had once been her mouth as she rammed the foot-long hunting knife straight up Chuck's ass to the hilt...and twisted.

Alex watched Chuck's face undergo a rapid-fire

series of transformations. Rage. Shock. Puzzlement. Disbelief. Then, finally, pain. He never made a sound. He stumbled backward a few steps, almost tripping over Sarah, and grabbed at the hard rubber handle jutting between his legs like an obscene growth. Blood torrented down his inner thighs like crimson diarrhea, soaking his jeans so that it looked like his bladder had burst. Hell, maybe it had, judging from how far in the blade was. Chuck fell on his knees, raising up puffs of dust, then toppled onto his side, writhing like an impaled worm. The ground beneath him turned to red mud.

Alex hardly noticed Chuck's dying convulsions. He had eyes only for Sarah. Beautiful, blood-sodden Sarah. Looked like Chuck had worked her over every bit as badly as he had Alex. Her intestines trailed behind her like a puppet's forgotten strings. It was impossible to count the wounds on her face, which was nothing more than a mask of blood. Her left eye was gone, leaving behind nothing but a gouged-out, gore-crusted socket. The crotch of her jeans was a mangled mess, and Alex didn't even want to imagine the things Chuck had done to her.

Instead, he marveled at her force of will, an absolutely stunning display of desire. She had crawled from the house all the way out to the barn—over one hundred yards—with her guts unraveling like party streamers while she left a trail of gore behind her like a slug's slime slick. She had gone through hell to reach him, and in her suffering lay the answer to his question. Right or wrong, theirs was true love.

She slowly climbed to her feet, clutching at him with fingers filleted of flesh. He and Sarah looked deep into each other's eyes, a visual connection every bit as intimate as the carnal embraces they had shared the last few months. Her hacked-up lips sought his. "Kiss me," she whispered. At least, that's what he thought she whispered. It was so hard to tell since Chuck had split her tongue down the middle.

And so Alex kissed her. Kissed her with a passion that blew away his pain like ashes in the wind. All that mattered was this moment, the love in his heart, the woman pressed against him. From somewhere deep in her mangled throat, Sarah moaned as their mouths met, blood and saliva mixing into a thick syrup that neither of them seemed to mind.

———

Four days later, with hunger gnawing at her belly like a rabid rat and six piglets wailing for milk, the sow busted out of the pen and went looking for food. It didn't take her long to find the three bodies behind the barn, sun-roasted meat rotting on the bones. She took a bite. Then another. And another.

Soon after, the crows came and picked the skeletons clean.

SACRED CREED

Vengeance is mine; I shall reward
Sin smoke whispers through dead man's eyes
Dimension's distance rides a scream
Wrapped in the shroud, innocence dies

Shadowed light of corpses and moon
And the steel through life rips and rends
Celestial clouds; Heaven's throne
Thunder's voice Creator shall send

Crimsoned marble and crypts of flesh
Silken threads surrendered to the moon
No demon fangs or Lucifer
Only God and seraphim croon

Welcome, children, to paradise
No blood-dripped streets of angel's hair
Frolic, caper, dance with the saints
Mind not the rough tongue of despair

Reaper, slayer, foul foe and fiend
Enter the mass of darkest night
Beg of the earth, weep to the storm
Revenge imminent, sin set right

Selfish vengeance, guarded justice
Sacred saints and holy tongues tell
Desecrater, surrendered soul
By sacred creed, you'll burn in Hell

SANITY'S TWITCH

AUTHOR'S NOTE

I went through a phase where the subject of insanity kept popping up in my fiction. This is my favorite story from that phase, with a smidgen of wish fulfillment—before marriage and kids, part of me dreamed the introvert's dream of becoming a hermit in a backwoods cabin with no human contact... though I would have left the cat behind. One of the first short stories I ever wrote, I was still in my teens when I banged this out on an old Brother word processor, which is probably considered an antique by today's standards.

I sit.

Naked.

With my gun.

Watching the mouse.

If anyone came along—an unlikely event, given my remote location deep in the Adirondack Mountains—seriously, my location makes Loon Lake look like a bustling metropolis—and asked me why I'm sitting here, I would give them a simple answer. Because it's easier than standing. Sometimes I watch this damn mouse for hours, and my old legs ache if I stand too long. I'm not as young as I used to be. For that matter, I'm not young at all.

I used to wear clothes, but now I don't bother. Why wear clothes if no one ever sees you? God doesn't care, the mouse doesn't care, and I'm pretty sure Tabby, short for Tabitha, doesn't care. Matter of fact, sometimes, when she wants some lovin', she even climbs onto my lap and rubs herself against my naked, wrinkled skin.

The gun, a battered old .303 British rifle that once belonged to my father, rests across the arms of the chair, pointed at the mouse hole. I'm bound and determined to kill that mouse. The little rat is driving me mad. It never emerges from its hole all the way. All I ever see is its tiny black nose or its twitchy little whiskers. But it comes out at night. I know it does because I can feel its beady black eyes watching me in the dark and good god, does that ever give me the creeps.

I don't even know how that damn mouse survives. The winters might be getting a little warmer up here in the Adirondacks, but not *that* warm. That rodent should have frozen to death by now. I mean, I'm so far back in the mountains that not even the hardiest hiker or deer hunter has ever stumbled across me. I used to live in the small hamlet of Bloomingdale, but that was fifteen years ago, before I turned my back on mankind and never returned. To hell with society and civilization. I'm happy in my tiny, one-room log cabin in the middle of nowhere. I came out here to escape, bringing only an axe, rifle, Tabby, and my Bible. The axe I used to cut down the trees to build this cabin, the rifle I used for protection and hunting, and Tabby I brought along for companionship.

Why did I bring the Bible? Well, you can run from man, society, and civilization, but you can't run from God. Jonah tried, and I sure don't want to end up like him, wallowing in whale puke, so I brought the Good Book. Besides, it gives me something to read when I'm not watching for the mouse. My favorite book is Song of Solomon. Its pages are worn and dog-eared, the ink so smudged I can barely read it, but that's okay because I've pretty much memorized it by now. I may be old, but the Song of Solomon still gets me hot n' bothered. I guess that's kind of sacrilegious, but I think God understands. After all, it's His book, and He included all that stuff about breasts and thighs. I'm just reading what He put there.

Maybe that's why the mouse glares at me from the shadows. Maybe popping wood over holy words is an unpardonable sin and this damn mouse is an avenging angel in rodent form, sent to punish me for my evil ways. Maybe it was sent to torment me into insanity until I suck on my gun, blow my brains out, and wind up in Hell for my wicked boners. No, no, that can't be it. Except for the insanity part. That may very well be true, 'cause this mouse is driving me bonkers.

"Bonkers" is what I wanted to name Tabby when we first got her since the fool cat was always running into walls and bonking her head. But Melissa wouldn't let me. Tabitha was the girl name she'd chosen when we were having our first, and only, as it turned out, baby. But our child turned out to be a healthy boy we called Eric, so the name Tabitha was still available when Eric, at the precious age of four, toddled in from his swing set with a tiny kitten in his arms. I remember that moment like it was only yesterday, him standing in the doorway, blond hair glowing like a halo as the morning sun streamed in behind him. He held the kitten out to Melissa. "Mommy," he said, "I found a kitty. Can I keep him?"

Not being much of a cat person myself, I was already plotting a dropoff at the Tri-Lakes Humane Society over in Saranac Lake. But before I could state my intentions, Melissa took the black-and-gray furball from Eric's arms and said, "It's a her, honey, and of course you may keep her. But first we have to give her a name."

Just then the kitten scampered from my wife's arms, hit the floor running, and bolted smack into the base of the stove. "Bonkers," I said. "Let's call the fleabag bonkers."

Melissa rolled her eyes at me, countered with, "How about Tabitha?" and the name stuck, eventually shortened to Tabby.

Tears drip down my grizzled cheeks. Even after fifteen years, the memories still hold a lot of pain. Seems like only yesterday I was holding Melissa, relishing the soft words she whispered to me in the dark as our darling son slept in the room down the hall, a tiny angel bathed in moonlight, comforted by the one-eyed teddy bear he called Poke because he was always poking his finger into the bear's empty eye socket and pulling out bits of cotton stuffing. Now all I have left is Tabby.

I look away from the mouse hole just long enough to glance at the cat. She's perched on my thigh, washing herself with a sandpaper tongue, but I know she has one eye locked on the mouse hole. Tabby has kept the faith right along with me ever since that rodent showed up five years ago. Oh, she acts real cool about it, like she couldn't care less if I ever kill the thing, but I know she's watching. Her aloofness is just typical feline attitude. Cats will be cats, I guess.

That's what I said to Melissa on our last day together. Tabby strutted into the yard with a dead bird dangling between her jaws, looking smug as Saint George when he slew the dragon. Melissa pretended to gag. I grinned at her and said, "Cats will be cats." Then I kissed her goodbye and waved as she drove off to take Eric to daycare, only a half mile up the road.

Only a half mile...yeah, sure, but tragedy knows no limits. I'll never forget the sounds. The piercing shriek of skidding rubber. The sharp crunch of crumpling metal. The jagged explosion of shattering glass. The hellish roar of savage flames. I remember running up the road to the intersection by Norman's General Store, all the heart-wrenching terror in the world rushing straight into my throat and forming a hard, vicious knot. "MELISSA!" I yelled. "ERIC!" I ran and prayed, my thoughts flying as fast as my feet. *Dear God, don't let them die don't You dare let them die don't if You do I'll kill myself I swear I will I can't live without them oh please dear God don't let them die don't let them die...*

I never stopped praying, not even when I saw the

fiery wreck, not even when I found both their bodies lying on the sidewalk, flung from the crash. I begged for a miracle, for the power of resurrection, for God to reattach Melissa's head to her body. I begged Him to heal the gaping gash in little Eric's neck. I begged Him to make the blood go away and the flames stop burning. I begged Him not to make me stand over two graves and say farewell forever. But my pleas were useless, for on that dark day God wasn't listening.

So, I retreated, figuring as long as I was saying goodbye to the two people I loved most in the world, I might as well say goodbye to the world too. If I couldn't have my wife and son, I didn't want anybody. I didn't want to look at the clerk in the store when I bought milk and wonder why his son was in kindergarten while mine was in the ground. I didn't want to hear the priest at St. Paul's Church on Sundays tell me how good God is when I know He sometimes lets His children suffer. I didn't want to see the wedding pictures in the Adirondack Daily Enterprise and wonder why the man in the photo was allowed to have his bride when mine was taken from me by a drunk driver who walked away from the accident without so much as a scratch.

That's the real reason I became a hermit—to keep from killing the son of a bitch who plowed into Eric and Melissa. I was scared I would pass him on the street one day and be unable to control my rage. Deep down in the blackest depths of my grieving soul, I knew if I ever saw him, I'd kill him. There would be no stopping me. Even now, all these years later, I sometimes wish I had tracked the bastard down and put a bullet in his skull. But somewhere he has parents who love him just as much as I loved my Eric. I couldn't sate my thirst for vengeance by inflicting upon them the same agony their son inflicted upon me. I couldn't bring myself to avenge my loss by forcing them to stand over a son's grave as I had. So instead of killing the bastard, I fled from him.

The mouse, however, is another story. I *know* I can kill him. Look at those whiskers, twitching and taunting. God, I hate that! It's driving me mad! Come out, you little shit, and let me blow you straight to rodent hell. No salvation for your kind, pal. I'm not even sure there's salvation for me. But I *am* sure I'll feel a whole lot better when I blast your head off. C'mon, vermin, come out and play.

Tabby suddenly stops washing herself. I glance at her. She is staring at the mouse hole, intent as a sniper locking crosshairs on his prey. I look back at the mouse hole and...

...OH MY GOD HOLY CRAP AFTER *FIVE YEARS*...

...the little bastard's *OUT*...

...and it has the face of the drunk who killed my wife and son!

I raise the gun. "DIE, YOU MURDERING SONUVABITCH!" I scream. "DIE!"

I pull the trigger...

...just as Tabby lunges for the little rat.

My bullet blows Tabby's head clean off.

It just disintegrates, splattering bloody chunks of bone and brain everywhere. I watch in silence as my only friend writhes in death spasms. Gradually, through an icy fog, I hear the sound of mocking laughter. I look at the mouse, but it retreats back into its hole until only its black nose and twitching whiskers are visible. Tabby's headless corpse continues to thrash, as if frantically demanding burial, but that will have to wait.

For now, I sit.

Naked.

With my gun.

Watching the mouse.

SUCK A BUS

AUTHOR'S NOTE

"Suck a Bus" is my twisted version of the college-kids-go-to-a-cabin-in-the-woods-and-get-slaughtered trope. Originally titled "Blood Oath Broken," the name switch occurred when I revamped the original serious tone into something more humorous. Many a reader has called the story a "romantic horror comedy," and while maybe that shouldn't work, yeah, it kind of does.

I staggered into the Washington County Sheriff substation shortly after dawn, covered with blood and brandishing a shotgun in one hand and a butcher knife in the other.

A portly deputy with a handlebar mustache that would have been comical under different, less-tragic circumstances sat behind a rickety old desk, leaning back in his threatening-to-topple chair as he read a newspaper. I could see the headline emblazoned in big, black, bold letters across the top of the front page. "Mystery Madman Murders Again." The English major in me appreciated the alliteration.

You would expect a gore-drenched man walking into a police station with weapons to generate some sort of excitement, elicit some sort of armed response. At the very least, you would expect the cop to put his hand on the butt of his gun. But not this guy. The deputy—his gold name tag said T. White—calmly put down the paper, then folded his hands on his ample beer belly, arched an eyebrow at me, and said, "Son, it looks to me like you've got one helluva story to tell, so why don't you just park your carcass in that chair right there and get to telling." Other than the arched eyebrow, he seemed fairly unfazed by my state of bloodiness, my twelve-gauge, or my big-ass butcher blade. His aloof demeanor seemed to say, *Ho hum, another crazy sumbitch with too many weapons and too few brain cells that I have to deal with.*

I sat down in the chair in front of his desk, laid the shotgun across my lap, and thought about setting the knife down on Deputy White's desk but figured he probably wouldn't appreciate fresh blood all over his official papers, so I decided to just hold on to it while I told him my story. And I did tell him. Told him everything. Even the part about what happened to Sheila in the cemetery. Even the part about all the killing.

As he suspected, it was one hell of a story.

"It all began yesterday..." I said.

———

Gary blew into my dorm room like a hot-wired bundle of barely bridled energy, a five-foot-ten cyclone clad in blue jeans and a sweatshirt emblazoned with our college logo, and flopped down on the bed beside my open suitcase. "Whatcha got?" he said cheerfully as he promptly began riffling the suitcase's contents. Nothing was sacred to Gary.

"Hey," I protested, "get your grubby paws out of my boxers."

"Oh, boy." He grinned wickedly. "What do we have here?" He pulled a box of condoms out from underneath a pile of my socks. My cheeks flamed red as he made a big show of reading the box. "Ribbed for her pleasure, eh? Never let it be said that Big Jim Daddy doesn't know how to treat a girl right." He tossed the Trojans back in the suitcase, then tossed me a pitying look that made me want to punch him in the face even though he was a friend. An irritating friend, sure, but a friend, nonetheless. "Jim," he said, "why are you torturing yourself like this? You know she just wants to be friends."

"She hasn't said that." The words sounded hollow even to my own ears.

"She hasn't said *anything*," Gary replied, "and that says all you need to know. Face it, my blue-balled buddy, you've fallen into that dreaded 'pal' category, and being a girl's pal is like being stuck in quicksand. Once you're in, you can't get out."

The "she" we were referring to was Karen Blake, a blonde-haired angel with girl-next-door good looks and the kind of curves that belonged in a Victoria's Secret catalog. She and I had grown up together in the small town of Harker Falls, a close-knit farming community in upstate New York. Her father was the pastor of the local Baptist church, but unlike most preachers' kids, Karen had never rebelled against her religious upbringing. She still believed and clung tenaciously to her faith, though college had shaken some of the strictness out of her. We'd been inseparable practically since we were born, and I had loved her since… well, forever. Sometimes I thought my feelings were reciprocated, other times I wasn't so sure. Sometimes I think even God Himself must be baffled by the mysteries of a woman's heart.

"Friends make the best lovers," I said, closing my suitcase to prevent Gary from pawing through the rest of my stuff. God knows I didn't need him to find the letter I'd written to Karen, confessing my deep feelings for her. I would never hear the end of it. "And as for the condoms," I continued, "well, hey, it never hurts to be prepared, right?"

"What a good little Boy Scout you are." Gary bounced up off the bed as if his butt was made of springs. "Think the others are ready to turn this campus into nothing more than a fading image in our rearview mirror?"

"They better be," I said, "because we're leaving in less than ten."

"Who put you in charge?"

I grabbed my suitcase and headed for the door. "I'm driving."

Gary grinned. "Gotcha." He followed me out of the room, closing the door behind him. As we took the stairs down to the parking lot, Gary said, "We're really not bringing Mary Jane on this trip?"

I sighed in exaggerated exasperation. This was

about the hundredth time I'd had this conversation with him. "No weed," I said. "Karen doesn't like the stuff, and since this weekend was her idea, we're going to respect her wishes. No drugs, no booze, those are the rules."

"Translation: no fun," Gary said, but his tone held no quarrel. "At least we'll be safe from any crazy psycho killers running around out there in the woods."

"Huh?"

"C'mon, man," Gary said. "You've seen the *Friday the 13th* and *Halloween* movies. Crazy killers always do the slice n' dice on people who are smoking weed or getting drunk."

I was something of a horror film buff myself. Everyone in the group was, to one extent or another, one of our common bonds. "Actually," I countered, "Jason Vorhees, Michael Myers, Freddy Krueger—even that little bastard Chucky—they all butchered plenty of people who weren't high or drunk. Besides, the biggest no-no in those movies is having premarital sex, and I'm pretty sure you and Sheila will be engaging in that little bit of nastiness this weekend."

Gary grinned. That grin had gotten him into more girls' pants than I cared to know. Not that getting into Sheila's pants was a tough trick for any guy. "You betcha," he said. "Guess that means if a big bad slasher is stalking the woods, Sheila and I will be the first to buy the farm, and your virginal princess will be the sole survivor." He let out a long sigh of exaggerated pleasure. "Ahhh, but what a way to go, lying between the legs of a beautiful woman."

"What lies between Sheila's legs will probably kill you faster than any psychopath," I muttered. We had reached the bottom of the stairs. I used my hip to push open the door that led out to the parking lot. "And hey, what makes you so sure Karen is a virgin?"

Gary snorted. "Yeah, right."

I could see the rest of the group—Karen, Sheila, and Rick—clustered around my station wagon, a beat-up-and-badly-battered '85 AMC Eagle with a rather severe stalling tendency. The only reason we were taking it on this trip was because of its storage capacity and four-wheel-drive capability. The rut-ravaged road leading up to the cabin we were staying at this weekend was one rough mother. "Really," I said, heading across the parking lot toward the others, "Karen has never said if she has or hasn't."

"Trust me," Gary said. "I can smell unporked pussy like a cop can smell a donut, and that little filly is pure, grade-A virgin."

I rolled my eyes. "Whatever."

"Fine, don't believe me," Gary said. "I'll ask her on the trip and prove it to you."

I glanced at him to see if he was kidding but knew he wasn't. If something was inappropriate, out of bounds, taboo, you could bet the last lint-covered nickel in your pocket that Gary would go there. Still didn't stop me from saying, "You will do no such thing."

Gary winked. "Watch me."

We walked up to the group, and I set my bag down on the ground so I could fish the car keys out of my pocket. Karen immediately gave me a quick hug and peck on the cheek. From somebody else, it might have meant something, but if I had a dime for every kiss on the cheek Karen had given me during our twenty-plus years of friendship, I'd make Donald Trump look like a piss-poor pauper. It meant nothing, regardless of how much my heart wanted it to. I gave her a quick squeeze back. "Hey there, gorgeous," I said with a smile. Karen could always put a smile on my face.

Sheila wrapped her arms around Gary's neck, gave him a wet, sloppy kiss, then pulled back, her full lips twisted in a pout. "Hey," she complained, "how come you never call me gorgeous?"

"Because," Gary said straight-faced, "if the shoe doesn't fit, then you can't wear it."

I started to chuckle, then stifled it when Karen shot me a *don't you dare laugh* look.

Sheila's look was more of the *I can't believe you said that* variety. She smacked Gary on the arm. "You're such a jerk," she said. "You're so mean to me, I don't know why I put up with your crap."

Gary wrapped his arms around her, keeping her from retreating. "Because you love me," he said with that roguish grin girls found so irresistible.

Sheila fought his embrace for a moment, but it was just for show. As always, she had fallen victim to that devilish smile. A smile of her own swept across her face, and she leaned into him. "You're right," she said. "I do love you." She gave him a quick kiss on the cheek.

"If everybody is done with the mushy shit, can we hitch horse to wagon and haul ass out of here?" Rick, the remaining member of our little group, asked with his usual patented sarcasm. He wore a baseball cap, bill-backward, to cover his prematurely thinning hair and an extra-large sweatshirt to cover his ballooning waistline. Rick might not have had much luck with the ladies, but he had never met a Little Debbie's snack cake he hadn't instantly fallen in love with. He wasn't fat yet, but he had definitely turned off the healthy highway and driven a mile or two down gluttony lane.

I popped the hatch and began slinging bags into the back of the car. "Jeez, Karen," I said, hefting her bags, "did you pack enough? It's a weekend getaway, not a month-long vacation."

"Please be careful, Jim," she said. "My equipment's in there."

I stowed her bag gently. Breaking her expensive, high-end photography equipment would not be the best way to begin what I hoped would turn out to be a romantic weekend. The next bag I grabbed happened to be Sheila's. Not as heavy as Karen's, but heavy enough. "We'll be lucky if the car doesn't bottom out when we hit the trail up to the cabin," I muttered.

"I only packed the bare necessities," Sheila said. She began ticking them off on her fingers. "Clothes, boots, makeup, bug-spray..." She grinned wickedly. "And oh yeah, my vibrator. God, I hope I brought enough batteries."

Beside me, Karen blushed. Growing up a preacher's kid, self-service sexual devices probably hadn't been a common topic of discussion around the dinner table.

Sheila turned to Gary. "You brought condoms, right?"

Oh, no. I could see it coming from a mile away, like a cruise missile fired from a battleship and zeroing in on me. Gary opened his mouth and delivered the blow. "If I need any, I'll just borrow some from Jim. He packed a whole box. I'm not sure, but I think he bought the jumbo size. The box, I mean, not the condoms." I didn't have to look at him to know the grin on his face was one the devil himself would be proud to wear.

Karen turned to me. Her face was expressionless, impossible to read, which was saying something, given how long I'd known her. "You brought condoms?"

"Ribbed," Gary elaborated.

I shot him a look that let him know psycho slashers in the woods were the least of his worries because if he didn't shut his pie hole in about two-tenths of a second, I would kill him myself. "I, uh..." I floundered about for an answer, came up with zilch, gave it another shot anyway. "Well, I, uh..."

Rick butted in. "Are we leaving or what?" His voice was plaintive, whiny. He was probably thinking about the Burger King on the way out of town and how many Whoppers he could cram down his gullet. "The cabin ain't getting any closer with us standing around yapping."

"Karen, listen, it's not—"

She turned away. "Save it, Jim."

"Can we at least talk about it later?"

"What's to talk about?" She sounded pissed. It hurt to hear her that way. "You feel what you feel, and I suppose there's nothing you can do about it. Just don't expect me to like it. I mean, after all we've been through, and now you pull this crap?" She climbed into the front passenger seat and slammed the door a lot harder than was necessary.

I turned on Gary like a starving wolf on a wounded rabbit. "What the hell is wrong with you, man?"

He held up his hands as if warding off an actual blow. "Whoa, whoa, whoa! Sheath the claws, tiger. What the hell is your problem?"

"You're my problem, asshole!"

Gary mimicked an electronic buzzing noise, then said, "Wrong answer, please guess again." He gestured toward the car. "Your problem is riding shotgun, amigo. That little filly has got you all twisted."

"He's right, you know," Sheila said.

I flung some of my anger her way. "Did I yank your chain?"

Rick piped up. "C'mon, guys, I thought we were going to a cabin, not auditioning for *Days of our Lives*. Turn off the drama and let's scram."

"Relax," I growled, "Burger King's open 'til midnight." But I turned my attention back to the pile of luggage heaped beside the car and began chucking bags into the cargo hold. I told myself to be careful with Karen's equipment, but it didn't really matter because Gary's little revelation had mucked up any chance I had of convincing her that we should be more than friends. Hell, the way she had reacted, it looked like even our friendship could be on the ropes.

I lifted a long leather case, and even though I knew damn well what it was, I asked anyway. "What is this?"

"My shotgun," Rick said.

Gary asked, "What the hell for?"

I asked, "Where the hell'd you get it?"

Sheila asked, "Are you fucking nuts?"

Gary, never one to miss a chance to crack wise, said, "This is Rick we're talking about. He isn't fucking anything."

"Hardy-friggin'-har," Rick drawled. "To answer your questions, I'm bringing a shotgun to do some small-game hunting—squirrels, rabbits, cute little fluffy animals like that. It's my shotgun from home, and

I brought it back with me after summer break, snuck it into the dorm. And no, I'm not fucking nuts. Let me tell you what fucking nuts would be. Fucking nuts would be going out into the woods without a gun, my ignorant friends. Now, can we *please* get our butts in the car and get the car moseying down the highway?"

I just shook my head and slung the shotgun into the back of the car.

"You know having a gun on campus is a felony, right?" Sheila glared at Rick. "Besides, how can you even shoot a squirrel?"

"Easy," Rick replied. "You just aim the barrel at its head and pull the trigger."

I squeezed in the remaining luggage and closed the hatch. "Let's roll." As I settled into the driver's seat, I glanced at Karen. She pointedly looked out her window, head turned away from me. I sighed, turned the key, and within thirty minutes—and one stop at Burger King—we were on the highway out of the city with a four-hour drive ahead of us. With a little luck, we would make it there just before dark, which would work out perfectly, since Karen wanted to photograph an old cemetery near the cabin using only moonlight, no flash. It would be the thirtieth such cemetery she had photographed. Natural light nocturnal graveyard scenes were quickly becoming her trademark. She'd even been paid a pittance by some underground horror rag to do a front cover for them. I had bought the magazine and read it from cover to cover. I should have stopped at the cover, for Karen's photography had been the best part of the rag. As for the stories inside...well, I would have rather read used toilet paper. Then again, maybe the pages of the magazine *were* used toilet paper, for there had been an awful lot of crap on them. Still, it was a publishing credit for her, and that was a good thing. She had torn the cover off my copy and framed it. It hung on the wall in her dorm room, right above the desk.

I could have hung Gary right about now. I was still pissed at him over the condom incident. Unfortunately, his next play did nothing to improve my mood. He leaned forward and tapped Karen on the shoulder. "Hey, K," he said, "I've got a question for you."

I glared at him in the rearview mirror, the kind of stone-eyed killer's glare that I liked to think would make Freddy Krueger himself think twice about crossing me. "Gary," I said in my most threatening voice.

He ignored me. "It's kind of delicate," he said to Karen.

She half-turned in her seat to face him. "We're all friends here." I could have sworn she stressed the word *friends* just for my benefit. "So fire away."

"Well, we were wondering—"

"You," I interjected. "*You* were wondering."

"Me, we, you, who...who cares?"

Karen smiled. "Just ask the question already."

I was happy to see her smile. I wasn't so happy to hear the next four words out of Gary's mouth. "Are you a virgin?"

I silently groaned at his crassness and kept my eyes on the road.

"Why?" she asked. "Do you need one for a sacrifice or something?"

"Are you dodging the question?"

"I'm not dodging anything," she said. "The answer depends on what you consider sex."

Sheila piped up from the seat directly behind me. "That's pretty easy."

"Stop talking about yourself," Rick muttered.

Sheila ignored the cheap shot and continued. "You just insert tab A into slot B. Thrust. Repeat until desired results are achieved." She laughed sultrily. "Of course, some folks require less thrusting than others." I glanced in the rearview mirror in time to see her elbow Gary in the side.

"Whoa," Rick exclaimed. "Too much information."

"Well," Karen said, "based on Sheila's definition, then the answer is yes, I am a virgin."

I breathed a silent sigh of relief. The thought of Karen getting it on with another guy left a cold nest of prickles in my heart.

Sheila chose that moment to change the subject. "Hey," she said, "anybody watch the SyFy channel last night? They played a movie I'd never heard of. It was called *Succubus,* and it was about this female demon who seduced men and then killed them."

"Suck a bus?" Rick snorted. "Sounds like something you would do."

"Screw you," Sheila said, "and that's something I definitely will *never* do."

"See, there is a God."

The rest of the trip pretty much went like that, friendly bickering and back-and-forth banter with the occasional semi-serious conversation thrown in to break up the ribbing. I mostly just listened, part of my focus on driving and the other part on Karen, who still seemed decidedly cool toward me.

"You okay?" I asked her once.

"Fine," she replied, but her terse tone let me know what she really meant was, *Don't talk to me.*

It was after dusk when we reached Pike Hill Road, the desolate gravel road that switch-backed its way up the mountain. Just before the turnoff to the cabin, my headlights flashed across a white Dodge minivan parked on the side of the road. "Strange," I murmured, making the left hand turn onto the rugged mile-and-half-long trail that would take us up to our destination.

"What's strange?" Gary called from the back.

"Nothing," I said. "Just seems like a weird place for a minivan to be."

"Maybe they broke down," Sheila said. "Maybe we should go back, see if they need help."

"Didn't see anybody in it when we went by," I said, fighting the steering wheel as we jounced over ruts deep enough to make the Grand Canyon jealous. Every so often a rock would scrape the car's undercarriage, metal shrieking as the AMC Eagle protested its abuse.

"Well, it's dark," Sheila said. "Maybe you missed them."

"Right," Gary said. "It's dark. If there's anyone in there, they don't want to be seen, if you know what I mean." He lunged at her, burying his face in the crook of her neck and making loud, disgusting slurping noises.

"Get off me," she said, laughing.

"I'd rather you get me off."

"I wish you would both fuck off," Rick muttered.

Ten rut-ramming, skull-shaking, brain-rattling, bone-jarring minutes later, we reached the cabin. Dusk was but a memory, replaced by true night. Honest-togoodness darkness now loomed where before there had been only murky shadows.

I grabbed a flashlight from the glove compartment and headed around back to fire up the generator. Rick announced he would get the wood stove going. No surprise there. Rick was half a pyro. Hey, everyone needs a hobby, right? Gary, Sheila, and Karen began unloading the car.

The generator was in a small shed out back. I swept the flashlight's beam around the interior. Rusty gas cans were piled everywhere. Cobwebs clung to the corners, dangled from the ceiling. Bleached deer skulls were nailed to the walls, hollow sockets pooled with shadows, decorations of the most dubious sort.

The generator looked like its best days had been sometime during the Nixon administration. It took some serious coaxing, but after I worked on it for a few minutes, alternating between gentle persuasion and beating the snot out of it, the machine surrendered to my advances and rumbled to life. I exited the shed and walked back to the cabin, the rectangles of yellow light spilling from the windows, proof that the generator was doing its job.

When I got inside, it was evident that Gary and Sheila had claimed one of the cabin's three bedrooms while Rick had laid claim to the second one. No sign of Karen, but her bags were sitting on the floor. My bags, on the other hand, were MIA.

Gary and Sheila stumbled out of their bedroom, giggling in what could only be described as a naughty manner. I could see a faint hickey on Sheila's neck and debated whether or not to tell her she had forgotten to zip her fly. Nah, she'd feel a breeze soon enough. "Hey," I said, "where's Karen?"

Before either of them could answer, I heard Karen call from the third bedroom. "I'm in here, Jim."

"Seen my bags?"

"They're in here too."

Okay, my bags were in the bedroom, so apparently it was my room. But Karen was in there too, so maybe not. But Karen's bags were out here in the main room, so...hell, I didn't know what to think. Strange, very strange.

I looked at Gary, who shrugged. "Got me, partner. Go in there and figure it out."

Rick emerged from his bedroom with his shotgun in hand. "One bunny obliterator, locked and loaded and ready for action," he announced.

"That's not the only thing loaded and ready for action," Sheila said, giving Gary's crotch a lascivious glance.

I rolled my eyes, then fixed them on Rick. "Seriously, is that thing loaded?"

"Wouldn't be worth much if it wasn't."

"A loaded gun in the house?" Sheila snapped. "You're an idiot."

"And you're a slut. So what?"

I left them to the name-calling that made up the bulk of their friendship and went to the bedroom that might be mine, might be Karen's, but would most likely never be *ours*. I knocked on the door gently and then pushed it open.

My bag was open on the bed, and Karen was reading the letter.

My heart froze as if Old Man Winter himself had

punched a fist right through my chest and squeezed it with his arctic fingers. *The letter...oh god no, not the letter.*

She didn't even look up as I came in, just kept on reading. I wanted to scream at her, *Stop reading! For the love of God please stop reading!* But instead, all I said was, "Uh, Karen, what are you doing?"

I could see her eyes flicking back and forth, taking in line after line. "I found this in your bag," she said, a breathless quality in her voice. "It had my name on it, so I thought I should read it."

"Karen, exactly why were you going through my bag?" I spoke cautiously, trying hard to keep my voice free of any accusatory tone.

She didn't say anything, just finished reading the letter, then looked up at me. My heart had unfrozen. Now it trip-hammered in my chest, pounding faster than the fluttering of a hummingbird's wings. Tears glistened in her eyes, and at that moment, I would have murdered a nun to know if those tears were a good sign or a bad one. She finally spoke. "I was looking for your condoms."

"The condoms? For what?"

"So I could throw them out."

I closed the door, not wanting the others to hear our conversation. "Karen, I'm sorry I brought them. I didn't mean to upset you."

"I was going to throw them out so you wouldn't screw Sheila." She said it so quietly I wasn't sure I had heard her correctly.

"What did you say?" I asked.

The tears spilled down her face. She brushed them away. "You heard me. I thought you wanted to screw Sheila. I thought that was why you brought the condoms. Then I found this." She held up the letter and looked at me with those beautiful teary eyes. "I'm sorry, Jim."

It all clicked in my head with a speed that would have left a cheetah in the dust. When Gary had blabbed about the condoms in my bag, Karen hadn't been upset because she thought I wanted to sleep with her. She'd been upset because she thought I wanted to sleep with Sheila. She wasn't pissed at me because I wanted to take our friendship to the next level. She was *jealous* because she thought I wanted to be with someone else.

But that meant...

"Karen," I said quietly, "the letter. What did you think of it?"

She smiled then, the kind of smile that could have put God on His knees. "Jim," she said, "what took you so long to tell me?"

I wasn't even exactly sure how it happened, but suddenly she was in my arms, and that first kiss I had craved for so long was actually happening. Was it everything I had always hoped it would be?

Oh, you bet your ass it was.

Her lips were absolute magic, and I never wanted their spell on me to break.

Several eternities later, we parted, breathless, hearts racing as one, both of us smiling the kind of smiles that only requited love can bring.

"I have to get out to the cemetery," she said. "We can talk more when I get back."

"I love you," I said. I had always wanted to say it, wondered how it would feel coming from my lips. And how it felt was damn good.

"I know," she said, still smiling that precious smile. "I read your letter."

Truth be told, I was a bit disappointed that she hadn't said, "I love you," back but decided not to read too much into it. Maybe she figured the kiss had said it all.

Whatever. She might not have chosen to vocalize her feelings, but we still strolled out of the bedroom hand in hand, so clearly, she had no problem letting the rest of the gang know about us.

Us. I savored the word the way a wine connoisseur savors a glass of France's finest. No longer were we just Jim and Karen. Now we were "us." Together. A couple. It had all happened so fast I was still having a hard time believing it. I felt like a Buddhist who without warning finds himself in nirvana.

"Whoa, whoa, whoa!" Gary exclaimed, pointing at our clasped hands. "What the big blue Beelzebub is this?"

"This," I said, "is you proven wrong."

"Well, spank me silly and call me Sally."

Rick slapped him on the seat of his jeans. "Take that, Sally."

Sheila rushed forward with an excited squeal and hugged Karen. "I'm so happy for you two. Unlike some people"—she rolled her eyes toward Gary—"I never doubted you two would be great for each other."

"Hey," Gary protested, "I never said they wouldn't be great together, I said Karen would never want to be more than friends with him."

Karen smiled at him. "You can't be right all the time, Gary."

"And seriously, I'm happy to be wrong this time. Good for you two."

"Yeah," Rick grumbled. "Good for them. Looks like I'm the only one not getting laid tonight."

"Stick your dick in that shotgun," Sheila suggested. "See which of you blows a load first."

"I would love to stick around for all this gutter talk," Karen said, walking over to the window, "but I really have to get out to the cemetery and take some shots." She pulled back the curtain. The light of the full moon frosted the woods, giving everything a stark, otherworldly gleam. "It's going to be beautiful."

"I can come with you," I said.

Sheila snorted naughtily. "That's what all the guys say, honey. Trust me, it's rarely true."

It took me a minute to get it. Then I blushed. Not really sure why, given all the nasty discourse that was part and parcel of our little gang. Maybe because it was about me and Karen.

Sheila hooked her arm through Karen's. "I'll tag along with you. It'll give us some girl time. Maybe I can give you a few tricks that you can try out on Jim when we get back."

I blushed some more.

"Gee," Karen said, "I didn't realize this was the devirginization cabin."

I had thought I couldn't get any redder. I had thought wrong.

The girls gathered up the camera equipment and sauntered off into the night. The cemetery was just a short stroll over the nearest ridge, so I wasn't worried about them getting lost, especially with the light of the full moon to see by. Us boys broke out a deck of cards and began playing some down and dirty Texas Hold 'Em.

"I could really go for a joint right now," Gary said, tossing down what I assumed was a bad hand. Either that, or he had fallen victim to my rash bluff. I had raised him twenty without so much as a pair to back my play.

"Hold that thought," Rick said as I raked in my winnings. He darted into his room.

"Rick," I yelled, "if you brought weed when I told you this was a weed-free weekend, I'll have your nuts in a vise."

From his room, Rick yelled back, "I always knew you wanted my nuts, homie!" When he reappeared, there was no sign of any marijuana, but he was holding up a case of beer. "No bongs, boys, but I brought the beer!"

"That's what I'm talkin' about!" Gary enthused.

I was irritated. "You're a putz, you know that, Rick? You just can't respect anyone's wishes. This trip was for Karen, and all she asked was for it to be booze- and drug-free. Was that really too much to ask?"

"Actually," he said, handing a beer to Gary, "yeah, it was." He popped the tab, slugged down at least half the can, then belched noisily. "Besides," he continued, "I figure she'll be too busy screwing your brains out when she gets back to even notice we had a couple cold ones."

"Jerk," I muttered, but I knew I had lost the battle. I just hoped Karen wouldn't be too ticked when she returned. As for the screwing my brains out part, that was more than I even dared hope for. Besides, even if we did engage in that particular activity, I wouldn't think of it as screwing, I would think of it as making love. Cheesier than a Harlequin romance novel, I know, but when it came to how I felt about Karen, it was the stone-cold truth. Screwing was what Gary did with a slut like Sheila. Making love was what two people who cared about each other did, people like me and Karen.

About one hour, ten beers (between Gary and Rick), and fifteen hands of poker later, the girls returned. I was up about sixty bucks, but I immediately forgot about my profits when I saw the shaken look on Karen's face. She was glancing at Sheila worriedly, forcing my attention her way. At first glance, Sheila seemed normal. It was only after studying her for several moments I saw the change in her eyes, the predatory glint, a hardening of the edges and angles of her pretty face. The change was subtle, but it was definitely there. There was something different about Sheila, but it wasn't something you could exactly put your finger on.

Karen came over and hugged me. She felt cadaverously cold. "There's something wrong with Sheila," she whispered in my ear.

Sheila was pulling Gary out of his chair. "Hey, wait a sec," he protested. "I'm down forty bucks to Jim. Give me a chance to win back my money."

"What I have in mind can't wait," she said, then giggled. For some reason it reminded me of the nails-on-chalkboard laughter of the possessed women in the *Evil Dead* movies. It was about as attractive as a dead baby.

As Sheila dragged Gary into the bedroom, Karen guided me into my bedroom, hopefully *our* bedroom before the night was through. "Look at this," she said, holding out her digital camera, the viewing screen flipped open so I could see the picture.

The photograph had obviously been taken in the cemetery. Crumbling stone crosses marked the ancient graves, shrouded in shadows and moonlight, the latter limning everything with a silver, otherworldly glow. Clearly not afraid to mix the sacred with the profane, Sheila straddled one of the crosses so that the top of the upright beam jutted phallically between her thighs. Her head was thrown back, hair wild like the wind-blown mane of an untamed horse, the look on her face one of over-the-top ecstasy, orgasmic to the extreme.

But it was far from the most disturbing thing in the picture.

"What the hell is that?" I said, looking up at Karen.

"You tell me," she said, the look on her face hard to describe but a long, long way from happy.

I stared down at the digital photograph. Directly behind Sheila, almost enveloping her, was a human shape. Well, not so much a shape as the *suggestion* of a shape. Ghostish, for lack of a better word. It was definitely white, and though not exactly transparent, it wasn't exactly solid either. The shape's face was clearly feminine, but the actual features were gauzy, smoke-like, out of focus, as if whatever the shape was refused to solidify its features or concrete its dimensions. The woman's hair was long and just as white and translucent as the rest of her.

I studied the blurry face intently. It was hard to see, but at that moment I would have happily slapped my hand on a big ol' stack of Bibles and swore the look I saw on that spectral face was lip-licking malevolence.

The billion or so horror flicks I had watched during my twenty-one years on this earth had tried to capture the face of evil, but they had all failed pathetically compared to what I saw in this photo—pure evil, rawer than sandblasted flesh.

And it was standing right behind Sheila.

"What happened after you took this picture?" I asked.

Karen fidgeted. "It's hard to describe."

"Give it your best shot."

She looked at me, fear staining her gorgeous eyes. "That...woman...or thing...or whatever you want to call it...it just...went into her."

"What do you mean, went into her?" I asked.

"It went *into* her." There was a hysterical edge creeping into Karen's voice. "I don't know how else to say it. You know like at the end of *Raiders of the Lost Ark* when the Ark is opened and all those demons come out and fly through the Nazis?"

I nodded. Classic film with an unbeatable climax.

"It was like that," Karen said. "Only instead of passing *through* Sheila, this...thing...stayed inside her."

"So, you're saying she's possessed."

"That would be my guess, yeah."

"Any idea why it possessed her and not you?"

"Who knows?" Karen shrugged. "Maybe because I'm a virgin? Maybe all those horror movies are onto something."

"The virgin rule only applies in slasher films," I said, some part of me hollering that we were a couple of morons for applying man-made movie rules to a real-life supernatural event. That hollering part certainly had a legitimate point, but it didn't prevent me from barging on. "This is a possession we're talking about, and in the movies, the only thing that protects someone from being possessed is—"

We looked at each other and finished the sentence together. "—faith."

"That's it," I said. "You're a believer, Sheila isn't, so whatever that thing is, when it was selecting its victim, really only had one choice."

"But why?" Karen wondered. "Why possess her at all? What's the point?"

At that moment, Gary's scream ripped through the cabin, filling every nook, crack, and cranny with the sound of agony.

Karen and I both jumped, then bolted out into the main room of the cabin.

The door to Gary and Sheila's room flew open. Gary staggered out, clutching at his crotch. Blood pulsed between his fingers, splattering the floor. His face was a rictus of pain. "Fucking bitch!" he screamed, the profanity trailing off into a whimpering wail.

Rick jumped up from his chair so fast it toppled over. "What the hell!"

"Oh my god!" Karen said. "Gary!" Then she asked a stupid question: "Are you all right?"

"Bitch!" Gary snarled again. He stumbled forward, leaving a trail of blood on the floor behind him, banged his hip off the corner of the table, and fell like a drunk to the floor.

"Gary," I said, "where's Sheila?"

"Bedroom," he moaned, eyes closed, fingers still grabbing his groin in a way that would have been obscene if not for the blood spewing all over the place.

"What happened?" I asked.

Gary's eyes popped open, and he answered with an outraged, pain-fueled bellow. "SHE BIT MY DICK OFF!"

Silence. From all of us. What do you say to an announcement like that?

Rick broke it. "Oh, that is so fucking *wrong*, dude."

Sheila chose that moment to make an appearance. I suspect she would've said something witty like, "What's all the hubbub, bub?" except she couldn't talk with Gary's manhood sticking out of her mouth like raw kielbasa, gripped by grinning, red-flecked teeth as blood dripped from the ragged stump and spackled the slopes of her breasts.

Rick was freaking out. "Oh shit oh shit oh shit, is that what I think it is? Is that his dick, oh god, is that his dick is that his dick in her mouth oh shit oh shit, the bitch bit his cock off just bit it right off oh shit oh shit..."

"Snap out of it," I said. His yammering hysterics were already sawing on my nerves.

"Fuck you, man. Do you see what I see? His damn dick, man, his dick she bit it off, oh god oh shit..." He ran into his room and returned holding the shotgun.

"The hell you planning on doing with that?" I demanded.

"Keep that psychotic skank away from me," he said. "I'm not losing my junk."

"No," I snapped, "you're losing your damn mind."

"I don't care about my mind!" he shrilled. "I care about my dick!"

Karen just stood there, staring at Sheila, completely stunned.

Gary still writhed on the floor, teeth gritted in pain, making the kind of noises that no man should ever have to make.

Sheila spat it out. It hit the floor with a meaty splat. Then she smiled an unholy smile, gave us each a long look, and then raised her foot.

Oh god, I thought.

She stomped down hard. It sounded like somebody taking a hammer to a slab of raw chicken. Pulpy gore spurted up between her bare toes. Her vile grin remained unaltered as she ground her heel into the chunky mess.

Then she turned toward Rick.

Maybe it was a trick of the light, but just for an instant I could have sworn I saw something, a face, maybe human, maybe not, lurking behind her eyes, as if the body belonged to Sheila but something else was inside her brain, sitting at the controls, pulling the strings.

She took two quick steps toward Rick, leaving sticky footprints in her wake.

Rick blew her head off.

Trapped inside the claustrophobic confines of the cabin, the shotgun's roar was a thousand times worse than the worst thunderclap I had ever heard. I swore my eardrums were ruptured like a sheet of rice paper struck by a semi.

The blast ruptured a whole lot more than Sheila's eardrums, however.

Her skull detonated as if she had swallowed a grenade. A sludgy stew of bone and brains splattered in all directions, leaving behind only a neck stalk spewing blood like a miniature version of Old Faithful. Sheila's hands reached up and grasped at the gory geyser, as if unable to comprehend where the hell her head had gone. In a movie, it would have been funny. In reality, it was sickening.

As if to prove that fact, Karen turned away and threw up.

With the sound of splashing vomit assaulting my ears, I whirled on Rick. "What the *fuck* is wrong with you?" I yelled. Part of me was in soul-curdling shock at what had just happened. Another part of me was angrier than a bull that's just been kicked in the gonads. And a third part of me was panicking like mad. I stomped toward Rick. "You just killed Sheila!"

Rick retreated from my advancing rage, seeming to shrink guiltily before my eyes. Or maybe that was just my imagination. "That wasn't Sheila, man!" he shrieked. "And you know it! That wasn't her anymore!"

"It's for damn sure not her now!" I snarled, moving in closer to him. Shock, anger, and panic continued to wage war within my guts, with no clear-cut winner emerging yet. "Her head is gone! *Gone*, you dumb shit. G-O-N-E. As in, no longer there."

"Piss off," Rick snapped. "I just saved all our asses, and you know it."

"You're not an ass-saver," I snapped back. "You're just a fucking murderer."

I knocked the shotgun out of his hands.

Big mistake.

The shotgun clattered to the floor and went off. Gary suddenly had worse things than an impromptu castration to worry about. Like the huge hole in his chest. Well, not really a hole. More like a crater, easily large enough for me to fit both my fists in, testimony to the power of a point-blank shotgun blast. His heart and lungs were nothing but mangled shreds of meat and tissue.

He didn't make a sound. Just looked at me in disbelief, closed his eyes, and died. The whole thing was just unbelievable. Three minutes ago, he'd been getting a hummer, now he was just a dead, dickless corpse. Funny how fast life could turn on you. Even funnier that I could think about things like that in the middle of this feces-hitting-the-fan scenario.

Finished puking up the Junior Whopper, onion rings, and vanilla shake she'd had for supper, Karen now huddled in the corner, clutching her knees to her chest, sobbing hysterically.

Rick glared at me. "Who's the murderer now, huh?"

"It was an accident," I replied, doing my best to hide the horror I felt over what I had inadvertently done, "and you know it. You, on the other, deliberately killed Sheila."

"I told you. It wasn't Sheila!" Rick snarled. "I had to protect myself. Protect *us*. Self-defense all the way, man. Perfectly justified."

"Yeah?" I said. "Well, tell that to the cops, see if it keeps them from slapping some shiny bracelets on your wrists and tossing you in the back of a squad car."

"Whoa, whoa, whoa," Rick said. "What do you mean, cops?"

"We've got two dead people on our hands, Rick. We have to call the cops."

"We can't call the cops. I'll go to jail."

Karen stopped sobbing long enough to say with uncharacteristic venom, "Jail is where you belong."

Rick jabbed a finger in her direction. "Shut up, bitch!"

"Hey," I said, "don't talk to her like that."

"Spare me the knight in shining armor, Casanova speech," Rick growled. "I'll talk to her any way I want. You're not the one she wants to put behind bars."

Karen climbed to her feet. Flecks of vomit speckled her lips. She wiped them away with the back of her hand as she approached Rick. "You decapitated an innocent woman—our *friend*—with a shotgun," she said with an iciness I had never heard from her before. "What makes you think you shouldn't go to jail for that?"

"You have to admit," I said, "that there *was* something wrong with her."

"You're taking his side?"

"No," I said hastily. "But the facts are the facts."

"Fine," she said. "I admit it. There was something wrong with Sheila. Still doesn't mean this trigger-happy troll had the right to blow her head off." She turned on her heel and headed for the bedroom. "I'm getting my cell phone and calling the police."

"Now hold on just a sec," I said. "Let's all press the pause button, cool down, and take a moment to think about this."

"There's nothing to think about," Karen said.

Rick moved faster than I had ever seen him move, committed to his course of action long before I had a chance to react. With a speed bordering on superhuman, he plucked a big butcher knife from the set on the counter and lunged toward Karen.

I had time to shout, "Rick, no!" and then "Karen, look ou—" before the sharp, heavy point of the blade plunged into her back right between the shoulder blades.

Frantic, I bent over and grabbed the shotgun.

Rick snarled, "You're not putting me behind bars, you sanctimonious bitch."

I stood up. Brought the shotgun to my shoulder just as Rick shoved the blade all the way in, burying it to the hilt. Then he backed away, legs wobbling weakly, as if he suddenly realized the terrible thing he had just done.

Karen turned toward me, grimacing in shock and pain. She had been completely skewered by the knife, the point popping out between her breasts, dripping with bloody filaments of heart tissue. Or maybe it was lung tissue. I didn't know the difference. I wasn't a medicine major. Didn't matter. Either answer was horrifying.

Rick pivoted to face me. Hysteria scored his face as if dug in by invisible talons, but there was honest to God regret in his eyes now as well.

Too fucking bad. Too fucking late.

Rick saw it coming. "Jim, no, wait..."

I killed him. One shot, right into his soft belly. So many emotions whiplashed through me that I couldn't even comprehend them all. Vengeance. Rage. Sorrow. Horror. Disbelief. Shock. Disgust. Guilt. A smorgasbord of feelings ripping at my soul as I watched Rick's guts blow open. I tried to pinpoint just one feeling as chunks of Rick's intestines pinwheeled through the air, but it was impossible. Not even the smartest shrink in the world could have figured out how I felt right then and there because *I* didn't even know how I felt. Within mere minutes, my world had been shattered. I had seen the unnatural, or supernatural, or whatever that white thing behind Sheila had been. I had watched Rick blow her head off. I had accidentally killed Gary. I had watched Rick stab Karen. I had killed Rick, this time the killing no accident.

And now...

Now I had to hold the woman I loved in my arms while she died.

Karen collapsed just as I reached her. I caught her before she hit the floor. I sank down into a sitting position and cradled her like a newborn baby, careful not to jostle the knife impaling her like a pin through the thorax of a displayed insect.

I kissed her. There was blood on her lips, but I kissed her anyway. My heart broke when she kissed me back. Even through her pain, even through the grim knowledge that she was just moments away from death, she cared enough to kiss me back. The tears streamed helplessly, hopelessly down my grief-stricken face. What was I going to do without her? The others, sorry as I was to see them die, I could live without if I had to, but not Karen. Sheila, Gary, and Rick had been friends, but Karen had been my love, and without her in my life, I didn't know how to go on. Wasn't sure I wanted to.

She was trying to say something. At first I thought she was asking to make out, which seemed like a really odd request from someone on the brink of dying, but then she said it again and I realized I had misheard her.

"Take...it...out," was what she had said.

I gave her a long look. "Are you sure?"

She nodded.

I didn't want to do it. It would hurt her and that was the last thing in the world I wanted to do. Worse, I knew when I pulled the blade out, it would be like pulling the drain plug in a full bathtub. The blood would come rushing out, and she would be gone far more quickly than if I left the knife in place. But how wrong would that be, leaving the knife inside her just to buy myself a few extra moments?

No, sometimes the right thing to do is hurt the ones you love the most. Like right now.

I reached behind her, fingers closing around the handle of the knife, flexing to get a good grip. I wanted it to come out in one quick, smooth yank, not prolong the pain.

"Ready?" I asked.

She didn't answer. Just closed her eyes.

I didn't wait. No deep breath, no silent prayers. I just pulled with everything I had.

She tensed as the knife came free but didn't cry out. The sickening sensation of metal sliding through meat and bone was transmitted to my hand, curdling something deep in the loneliest part of my soul. But I didn't waver, and in the blink of an eye, it was over.

Blood gushed everywhere.

I tried to stop it. I prayed lots of silent prayers now, begging God to stop the bleeding, but apparently God wasn't in the mood today to do a divine stitch job on a punctured lung or sew up a pierced cardiac muscle. No, judging from the ghastly river of blood spilling out of Karen, the only thing God seemed in the mood for was letting her die and adding another angel to his heavenly legions. Part of me wanted to scream, *Thanks for nothing!* But I knew Karen wouldn't have approved, so I bit my tongue, part of me really hoping God couldn't hear my thoughts.

"Jim."

I looked down at her. She smiled up at me. Beyond that smile, I could see the end, so close, so near, unstoppable. I had thought my heart was already broken, and maybe it was. But it broke again at that moment.

She said the words I had craved for so long. "I love you, Jim."

"I love you too," I said through my tears, but she never heard me. She was gone.

I sat there with her in my arms through the night, hour after hour ticking by with metronomic relentlessness, rolling steadily toward the dawn. Sometimes I wept hard, sometimes I was stonily stoic. Sometimes I bent my head to look at her, sometimes I simply stared straight ahead. Sometimes I wanted to go on living life for the both of us, sometimes I wanted to slash my wrists until the severed veins spilled out like sodden spaghetti. Sometimes I cursed God for taking her, sometimes I begged Him to take care of her now that she was on the other side. A lot of back and forth that night, but one thing I knew for certain as the pendulum swung between emotional extremes was that I had loved her, and she had loved me.

Maybe it was enough.

———

"I waited until dawn," I told Deputy White, finishing my story, "then drove straight here."

The deputy hadn't so much as twitched the entire time I'd been talking. Only the blinking of his eyes and the rise and fall of his chest proved he wasn't a corpse. A prime example of absolute stillness. Now he unfolded his hands and leaned forward in his chair. I noticed the very tips of his handlebar mustache were trembling slightly, as if stirred by sonic vibrations. "Son," he said, "that is one hell of a story. A real humdinger."

Relaying the tragic events of last night had left me utterly exhausted. I felt broken, beat down, battered, and bruised by the cross crushing down on my shoulders. It was the cross of shock, the cross of loss and rage and grief and guilt. It was a heavy cross, one I knew I would be carrying the rest of my life. I had no idea how I would do it, either. I leaned forward, burying my face in my hands, shoulders slumped beneath the overwhelming weight of it all. I felt like I should cry, but all my tears had been shed last night as I held Karen's body in my arms. I had no tears left to give.

"It's also," White rasped, "complete and total bull."

I raised my head, surprised by the change in the deputy's tone.

White was pointing his duty weapon at my face. Some kind of ugly black automatic. I could no more discern the difference between a 9mm or a .45 or a .40 than I could tell the difference between a Methodist or a Presbyterian or a Wesleyan. All I knew was that the cyclopean muzzle looked like the gaping maw of Hell. I saw that the finger Deputy White had curled around the trigger was trembling even worse than his outdated mustache. *Holy shit!* I thought. *I'm just a finger twitch away from dying and don't have a clue why.*

"Sir," I said cautiously, "with all due respect, what the fuck?"

"Shut your mouth," White snarled, hostile as hell. "I know who you are." With his free hand, the one not holding the gun, he pounded on the newspaper draped across his desk, finger stabbing at the Mystery Madman Murders headline. "That's you. You're the mystery murderer who's been killing all those people 'round these parts."

"Sir, seriously, listen to me..."

"SHUT UP!" he bellowed, eyes bulging with fury. I could tell he wanted to pull the trigger, wanted to pull it real bad. "That white minivan you so conveniently mentioned parked on the side of the road? It belonged to the sheriff's wife. We found her and their ten-year-old daughter in it late last night." His words came out hard and fast, like the bullets he wanted to pump into my face. "His wife had been butchered. With a knife. Just like the knife you've got in your hand there. Same way as all those others you killed. Eyes gouged out, throat cut, belly sliced open, blood an' guts everywhere. We found the little girl in the back under a pile of her mother's intestines. Somebody blew her face off with a shotgun. Just like the shotgun you got there." His eyes narrowed to icy, glittering slits. "Yeah, I know who you are." I suddenly realized his trigger finger had stopped trembling.

Oh shit.

"Deputy," I said, "you've got it all wrong."

"Maybe," Deputy White said, and then he shot me. Right smack in the face.

The bullet hit me in the upper lip and bored through the bottom regions of my brain. I felt a terrible shattering sensation and then my head snapped back, and I was staring up at the ceiling fan, paddles oscillating slowly, stirring specks of dust.

No pain. Not yet anyway. Maybe it would come. I stared at the ceiling fan and waited.

Soon the fan disappeared, and I saw the face of Heaven.

Karen.

She was smiling at me.

There was blood on my teeth.

Didn't matter.

I smiled back.

ARMAGEDDON'S GALLOWS

Clouds wrap the world like a shroud around a desiccating corpse
and the blazing eye is blinded in a darkening veil of grief
until only shadows mourn for the fallen lover

Sun blades razor the dust with fiery edges and sizzling wounds
and blood sweat stains the dying brow as the victim burns
like a witch damned on judgment day

Lightning slashes like the lashing tongue of Lucifer
as jagged knives rip the swollen flesh of the celestials and blood falls
like tears onto the wounded soul, drowning it like Atlantis lost

Rain bloodies the wounded creation of grieving gods
while the black crystals of Gehenna prophesy a flooded land
and a welter of sins washed in an angry flow of raging sorrow

The moon carves its narcotic magic into the pinpricked
night
while its seeping flesh rots on its bloated body and there is
no grin
as the Reaper's breath summons eternal murder

Chaos echoes and four horsemen thunder toward destiny
as a crimson tide rises to slay the steeds of millennium's
armies
yet on that day no light from Hell but from the eyes of
dawning resurrection

CHANCE DANCE

AUTHOR'S NOTE

"Chance Dance" represents a convergence of three of my obsessions at the time: westerns, horror, and poker. You could argue that the message, symbolism, and imagery of "Chance Dance" is heavy-handed, and you would not be wrong.

THE LAST CHANCE SALOON, DRY GULCH, WYOMING, 1878

Smoke from John "Lucky Draw" Thefton's hand-rolled cigarette drifted up into his dark eyes, but years of smoking had immunized him to the acrid sting. He didn't even squint against the gray haze, just kept his eyes on the cards in his hand. A ten, jack, queen, and king, all spades, and a useless four of hearts.

He glanced at his opponent. The face of Gene

Simper, a cowboy from the Bar T Ranch, was like a time-worn tombstone, revealing nothing. Thefton's gaze dropped to the mound of money in the middle of the knife-scarred, booze-stained table. About two hundred greenbacks, give or take. Not the richest pot he'd ever played for—that had been a year or so ago on a riverboat in Louisiana—but more than enough to get his blood pumping with the desire to win.

This being Five Card Draw, all he had to do was toss away his four of hearts and draw the ace of spades to complete a Royal Flush, the highest possible hand in poker. But the odds of that...well, he had a better chance of kicking a mule over the moon.

Then again, they didn't call him "Lucky Draw" for nothing.

"C'mon," Simper growled. "I ain't got all day. Gotta get back to the Bar T soon."

"Poker's not a game to be rushed," said Thefton. "If you were in such an all-fired hurry, you should've stayed outta the game."

"Your opinion means 'bout as much to me as the horse shit on the bottom of my boots," Simper retorted. "Just bet or fold already."

Thefton slid two ten-spots into the pot. "I'll see your twenty."

"'Bout damn time." Simper picked up the deck. "How many?"

Thefton threw down his four of hearts. "One."

Simper dealt him a single card. Thefton left it where it fell, face down in front of him. Simper tossed away two cards and drew two new ones from the deck. "Your bet," Simper said.

Not bothering to look at the card he'd been dealt,

Thefton pushed a stack of bills into the middle of the table. "Hundred."

"What the—! Thought this was supposed to be a friendly game!"

"Ain't nothing friendly 'bout poker," Thefton said. "If you ain't got the guts for it, you should fold, tuck tail, and run on home."

"Kiss my ass." Simper threw a fistful of tens into the pile. "I'm callin' you."

Thefton spread his four cards—ten, jack, queen, king—out on the table beside the face down fifth card.

"Ain't no good without the ace." Simper tried to sound belligerent but looked worried.

Thefton turned over his last card.

The ace of spades.

Simper's mouth fell open as his cards tumbled from suddenly limp fingers. In any other game, it would have been a winning hand—full house, kings over nines—but not tonight, not against Lucky Draw Thefton. Anger flickered across Simper's face. He powered to his feet, chair toppling over with a crash. "You cheatin' sonuvabitch!" He reached for the six-gun slung at his side.

Before he had even cleared leather, Thefton's pearl-handled Colt .44 was aimed right between his eyes. "Don't be a fool," Thefton said. "You ain't even close to fast enough."

Simper let his revolver drop back into its holster, but his eyes blazed with hostility. "One day, Thefton, your luck's gonna run out. You'll go up against someone better'n you, someone luckier'n you, someone who'll clean you out right down to your last penny and put a bullet in your belly. I just hope I'm there to see it when it happens."

"And I thought this was supposed to be a friendly game," Thefton drawled. "Care for another hand?"

"Forget it. Find another sucker to cheat."

"I've never cheated at poker. Call me lucky, skilled, or whatever, but don't call me a cheat. I wouldn't dishonor the game like that."

Simper rolled his eyes. "Listen to yourself. You talk about poker the way preachers talk about God." He turned away, shaking his head. "I need a drink."

As Simper bellied up to the bar to nurse his woes, Thefton quickly counted his winnings. Four hundred and twenty-seven dollars. Not a bad night's take, more than enough to replace the horse he'd left as buzzard bait about nine miles outside of town after it got bit by a rattler. But it would never be this good again, not in this town. Once word of his win against Simper spread through Dry Gulch, no one would risk playing against him. Might as well pack his bags tonight, buy a new horse in the morning, and ride on to the next town. Such was the life of a professional gambler—rich, but rootless.

And don't forget loveless, he reminded himself.

His vagabond life left no room for romance despite the women he met in his travels. Any relationship would be fleeting at best, and while ruthless at the card table, he had no wish to leave a trail of broken hearts behind him, so he abstained from female company. It was the one thing missing in his life, the only regret he had about the profession he had chosen. The thrill of victory came with a side order of loneliness.

"So why not solicit the services of soiled doves?"

The voice pulled Thefton's gaze up from the stack of coins and bills. A well-dressed, middle-aged man sat across from him in the seat recently vacated by Simper. *Where the hell'd this guy come from?* he thought. *I didn't even see him come in, let alone sit down at my table.* Aloud he asked, "What?"

"Soiled doves," the man repeated. "Whores, to indulge in the common vernacular. If you crave female companionship, why not partake in their offerings?"

"What makes you think I want a woman?" Thefton plucked the cigarette from his lips, dropped it on the floor, and crushed it under his boot heel. "Who are you anyway?"

"I apologize. My name is Lucas Cypher. And you are..."

"Why don't you tell me? Apparently, you can read my mind."

Cypher smiled gently. "No, no, nothing like that, Mr. Thefton."

"Then how do you know my name? We've never met."

"Your reputation precedes you, sir."

Thefton was getting tired of this guy. "Anybody ever tell you that you talk like a jackass?"

The smile wilted from Cypher's face. He started to stand. "I apologize for wasting your valuable time. I believed you were seeking a game of poker, but obviously you are only interested in cheap insults at the expense of a harmless stranger. Good evening, sir."

"Wait." Thefton reached out his hand as if to literally hold Cypher in his seat. "Sorry. It's been a rough couple of days, and you just took me by surprise, knowin' what I was thinking at that exact moment."

Cypher's smile returned. "It's my gift."

Thefton quickly gave him the once-over. Cypher wore an immaculate three-piece suit, the black cloth clean of dust and dirt. His white shirt showed no sign of sweat stains, a remarkable feat for this time of year in Wyoming. Hair as black as his suit swept straight back to reveal a handsome but sharp-edged face with thin red lips and a nose curved like a hawk's beak. But by far his most unique feature were his eyes, colored a startlingly pale blue, almost like slivers of ice. Skilled at reading people, Thefton searched for menace in Cypher's steady gaze but found none. Satisfied with what he saw, he said, "So you want a game?"

Cypher nodded. "Gambling is one of my many vices."

"You any good?"

"I suggest you deal the cards and discover that for yourself."

"You got money?"

Cypher patted his breast pocket. "Right here." He then reached down and lifted a brown leather satchel onto the table. The satchel had strange markings on it that reminded Thefton of some Egyptian hieroglyphics he'd seen in a book once. "And I have additional funds in here."

Thefton inwardly let out a long whistle. *A bag full of money...this fella's a serious player.*

"Is that acceptable?" Cypher asked.

"Sure."

"Then let's play, shall we?"

For the next two hours the cards flew, and Lucky Draw Thefton lived up to his name. If Cypher had a pair of jacks, Thefton had a pair of queens. If Cypher had a straight, Thefton had a straight flush. No matter what cards Cypher had, Thefton's were always better, so the cash continued to pile up on his side of the table. He glanced at Cypher. *I thought this guy was good.*

"I am good," Cypher said, once again displaying his eerie ability to read Thefton's mind. "Apparently you are superior."

"Didn't mean no offense."

"None taken, Mr. Thefton. You are an exceptional card player, and I am obviously outmatched." Cypher leaned back in his chair. "If things continue to unfold in this manner, you will soon need a bigger table. I understand why they refer to you as Lucky Draw. If I did not know better, I would suspect you of cheating."

"I never cheat at poker."

"I know. I can discern an honest man when I see one."

"Want more, or have you had enough?"

Cypher's ice-blue eyes narrowed slightly, and for the first time, Thefton saw there was something strange about that pale gaze. Shadows lurked behind Cypher's stare, as if his pupils concealed something unwelcome.

Simper wandered over from the bar and nudged Cypher's shoulder. "Hey, fella, take it from me, quit while you still have the shirt on your back. Thefton here's a stinkin' card shark."

Another shadow pulsed across Cypher's eyes like a storm cloud writhing across a pale blue sky. "Thank you for the advice, sir," he said, "but I do believe my luck is about to improve."

Simper snorted. "You're playin' against the king of luck, fella, but it's your funeral."

Cypher looked at Thefton. "One more game?"

"If you've got the money."

"I have something you desire more than money."

"There's nothing I want more than money."

Cypher snapped his fingers.

The batwing doors swung open and in walked the most beautiful woman Thefton had ever seen. Raven-black hair cascaded down to her shoulders in satin waves, framing a heart-shaped face and eyes of crystal blue, strikingly similar to Cypher's. Her figure was pure perfection, her crimson dress accentuating her upper body before flaring over her hips and down to the floor. She caught Thefton staring and gave him the kind of smile that could melt the coldest heart. As she crossed the rough plank floor, every man turned to watch her pass by, a goddess descended to walk among mere mortals. She went to Cypher's side and rested a hand on his shoulder.

"One game," Cypher said. "If you win, my daughter, Angelina, will be your companion until the day you die. Wherever you go, she will go. A more lovely and faithful companion you could never ask for."

Thefton felt trapped by Angelina's crystal eyes and alluring smile that promised so many delicious things.

"Think about it," Cypher continued. "You need never be lonely again. Angelina will stay with you forever."

Thefton knew bullshit when it was being shoveled, but he asked anyway. "And what happens if I lose?"

Cypher smiled that gentle smile of his...only this time it wasn't so gentle. "If you lose, your soul is mine."

"My soul?"

Cypher nodded. "Yes, Mr. Thefton, your soul. You

see, reading minds is not my only talent. I also collect souls."

"Sure you do."

Cypher leaned forward and unlatched his satchel. "Look and listen."

Thefton abruptly felt uneasy. For some reason, the last thing he wanted to do was look in that bag. He licked his lips, still cracked from his unexpected walk in the sun two days ago. His tongue was dry as desert sand. *For god's sake,* he chided himself, *it's just a bag.*

He leaned forward and looked inside...

...and then threw himself back in his seat with a scream. The flesh crawled on his bones, and his entire body shuddered like a man left naked in a howling blizzard. He stared at Cypher with haunted eyes and felt something deep inside himself going mad. He slowly became aware of the drool slobbering from his lips and the shocked stares of everyone in the room as his terrible cry echoed through the saloon. Still shaking like a leaf in a whirlwind, he wiped away the spit dangling from his trembling lips.

Cypher closed the satchel. "Souls," he said quietly. "My pride and joy. Are you prepared to wager yours, Mr. Thefton?"

Thefton knew if he lived to be a hundred, he would never forget what he had glimpsed inside Cypher's bag. He could feel it deep in his bones—no, beyond his bones, in that dark place beyond flesh and marrow.

"I am waiting, Mr. Thefton." There was a lilting, sing-song quality to Cypher's voice, but honed with a harsh edge. "Are you willing to wager your soul against the chance for everlasting love?"

Thefton fought for control and managed to stop

shaking. His mind pulled itself back from the brink of madness by coming up with a rational explanation. *A trick. That's all it was. He's one of those carnival magicians with a bag full of mirrors or something. No one can collect souls, and no bag can contain what I saw. So, get a grip, grab your balls, and let's do this.*

Cypher waited, eyes brimming with shadows. "Well?"

"Deal 'em," Thefton rasped. "But if you're screwing with me, I'll put a bullet right in your face."

"No need for threats, Mr. Thefton." Cypher dealt them each five cards. "If you win, Angelina really will be yours, and if you lose, your soul really will be mine."

Yeah, sure. I think you're not right in the head, fella.

Simper said, "Hey, Thefton, didn't I hear you talkin' 'bout this guy being able to read your thoughts? Sure you wanna play poker against a fella who can read your mind?"

Thefton picked up his cards as he replied, "It's one hand, winner takes all, best hand wins. No bluffing, no strategy. This hand is all about the luck of the draw, so doesn't matter if he can read my mind or not."

Thefton glanced at his cards, then did a double take. It was the same hand he'd held against Simper just three hours ago—ten, jack, queen, king, all spades, and a four of hearts. All he needed was the ace of spades and Angelina would be his. He looked up at her, and she smiled back, her ruby lips ripe and wet and hinting at forbidden desires. God, she was beautiful. He needed that ace. Sweat beaded his skin and stained his shirt with dark circles.

Cypher, on the other hand, seemed as cool as his

eyes. He didn't even bother to look at his cards. "How many?"

"One." Thefton threw away his four of hearts and received a single card in return. *Please, God, let this be the ace of spades.*

Cypher threw away two cards but drew only one.

"Hey," said Thefton, "you only took one card."

"I know. One is all I require."

Thefton shrugged. "Suit yourself." He looked at the card he had drawn. His heart dropped into his guts, which began churning like a nest of cold, roiling maggots.

Six of clubs.

Smiling, Cypher spread his cards.

Four aces.

The ace of spades lay on top like a black taunt. Thefton stared at the card, *his* card, and felt all his infamous luck flow out of him like blood from a slit throat. His stomach continued to churn, and he doubled over, sick and gagging, sweat dripping from his face onto the losing cards.

"You lose, Mr. Thefton," Cypher said. "Time to pay."

Thefton looked up, and his blood froze. Cypher's eyes were no longer arctic blue and stained by shadows. The ice had melted, the shadows vanished, and now those eyes glowed brimstone red. It was as if Cypher had gouged out his own eyes and embedded hot coals in the sockets. "No!" Thefton gasped. "Oh God, no..."

"Yessssssss..." Cypher's tongue teased the word into a hiss.

Glimpsing that tongue, Thefton would have sworn it was sleek and forked, just like the tongue of the rattler that had killed his horse two days ago. The beginning of his bad luck.

His hand inched toward his Colt. "What the hell are you?"

"I have so many names." Cypher's fingernails extended before Thefton's horrified eyes, curving into cruel claws that reached toward his chest as if to tear it open like a sack of grain.

Thefton staggered to his feet. His chair toppled over with a crash. Screaming so hard he thought his lungs would come out in hot chunks—"NOOOOOOOO!!!!!!"—he drew the .44 with a speed that would have impressed any gunslinger. Fear pumping through his veins, he slammed back the trigger and fanned the hammer. Flame and steel leaped across the table.

All six shots tore into Cypher's face. His cold smile blew apart like clay, ripping away the flesh in bloody ribbons to expose the dark, horrible creature beneath.

Thefton's fingers went limp. The gun clattered to the floor, spilling empty cartridges. His eyes bulged with shock. "What in God's name are you?"

Horns sprouted from the beast's skull and arced upward like deadly daggers. Its pupilless eyes stared at Thefton, and he saw his reflection in the blood-red glow. Razors filled the monster's mouth, and a serpentine tongue slithered among the blades. As the creature twisted slightly, Thefton saw small, membranous wings folded against the bony spine. The thing stank of sulfur, and its hide was singed and blackened. When the razored maw opened, the voice that emerged was raw and guttural, nothing like the smooth, cultured tongue of Lucas Cypher. "God has nothing to do with me, fool, and now He will have nothing to do with you either."

On the table, the satchel gaped open of its own accord and began thrashing like a starving wolf in the presence of a wounded lamb.

"No!" Thefton begged, but his pleas were useless. He felt something loosening inside him, something precious that felt like it was being snagged by giant fishhooks. Terror clogged his veins like thick black oil.

"You made a deal with the devil," the beast replied. "Now it's time to dance."

The agony hit him in one great crushing wave. Thefton fell to his knees, screaming as his chest split wide open as if someone had struck him with an axe. Blood exploded into the air and spattered against his eyeballs like raindrops. Pain beyond anything he could have ever imagined gripped him like a vise.

And then he was outside himself, looking down at his gushing body while a hungry force sucked him toward the satchel. As he slithered into the mystical bag and down into the abyss, he was snared by the unholy creatures he had glimpsed when he first looked into the satchel. The creatures that had driven him to the edge of gibbering insanity. Their gore-streaked claws sank into his soul as they swarmed over him, eyes wild and lusting for his pain, his screams, his eternal damnation.

The largest of the demons opened its mouth, crimson drooling from its fangs. "Welcome," it hissed, a hungry smile curving its pus-spotted lips like a stained scythe. "This is your lucky day."

And then the beasts began to feed.

BROKEN MIRROR

AUTHOR'S NOTE

"Broken Mirror" is a dark take on the fear of growing old, written long before I had any inkling what growing old felt like. It originally appeared in a horror rag called Night Terrors magazine, my first "professional" sale. Sure, if the 'zine had more than 300 subscribers, I'll eat my boxers with barbecue sauce, but back then, I didn't care. In fact, I still don't. It was a milestone in my writing career.

"Daddy, what are those lines on Grampa's legs?"

Josh Phearson put a hand on his six-year-old daughter Jessica's head and gently stroked her silken blonde curls as he gazed down at his bedridden father. Were it not for the subtle rise and fall of Sam Phearson's sunken chest, he might have been a corpse. The thought sent something cold slithering down Josh's spine, and he had to look away. Swallowing the golf ball-sized lump in his throat, he answered, "Those are called varicose veins, honey."

Jessica wrinkled her nose. "They're gross."

From the mouths of babes, Josh mused. "That's what happens when you get old, sweetie."

Jessica looked up at him, eyes azure and innocent. "Will that ever happen to you, Daddy?"

Josh heard the concern corroding her usually sweet voice. *She's afraid,* he realized. *Afraid that someday I won't be able to hold her, protect her, pick her up when she falls. My God, what am I doing to my little girl by letting my dying father stay with us?* "I don't know," he replied honestly, for Jessica had the keen ability to dissect any lie. "Maybe someday, if I live to be as old as Grampa."

"I don't want you to be old and ugly." Her voice quivered, the fear of a child facing something she couldn't understand. "I'm gonna pray to God that you'll always be big and strong. I'm gonna go pray right now." She turned and left the room, a tiny angel on a mission of mercy.

I hope He answers you, Josh thought. He and God hadn't been on speaking terms for over two years now, since the tragic farming accident had taken his mother's life. While putting a bullet in the brain of the rabid bull that had stomped and gored her to death, Josh had angrily vowed to God to never pray again and to never again set foot inside a church. If there was one thing Josh was good at, it was keeping his promises.

He turned his gaze back to his father, again struck by just how much like a corpse he looked. Dad's hair was white as sun-bleached bone and just as brittle, fanned across the pillow like a fallen spider web. His facial bones were prominent, cheekbones jutting starkly through folds of loose, wrinkled skin. Josh remembered his father once telling him that wrinkles were storylines, each one telling a tale, but now, staring at his dad's wasted body, Josh saw the wrinkles not as storytellers, but as ruts of decay. There was nothing noble or dignified about them. Old age was a demon, wrinkles the mark of its claws, torn into aging flesh as a foretaste of an imminent grave.

Josh continued looking at his father, knowing he was glimpsing his own future but vehemently refusing to acknowledge the fear and loathing it spawned in him. Dad's chest was a sunken ruin, ribs and sternum visible under the desiccated skin. A thin white sheet was draped over his loins like a flag on a coffin, but Josh had cleaned the results of his father's incontinence enough in the past year to know that hips and pelvic bones were equally prominent, even when smeared with feces.

He forced his eyes lower, taking in the thin, shriveled legs that looked so much like brittle twigs. A far cry from the thick, muscled limbs Josh remembered from his childhood when Dad would race him through golden fields and crystal creeks, the cool splash of the water a welcome relief from the warm summer sun.

Tears scalded Josh's eyes. *It's just not right. A man shouldn't have to watch his dad waste away like some rotting weed. Life's hard enough without having to be reminded that someday your daughter might have to wipe your ass because you'll be too weak to control your own bowels.*

How long he stood there, burning in his tears, he didn't know. But after some time, a withered, birdlike hand touched his wrist, and he heard his father's hoarse, croaking voice whisper, "Son."

Josh looked down and saw that his father's eyes were open, fixed on him in a deep, probing gaze that seemed custom designed to lay bare any and all secrets. Josh felt ashamed under that unwavering stare, but he couldn't help what lurked in his soul. He took his dad's hand, repulsed by its skeletal feel. "I'm here, Dad." He forced mock tenderness into his voice, furthering his feelings of shame.

"Son," his father repeated, unaware that his breath repulsed Josh, for it reeked of the Reaper. "Son, I'm sorry. I know what I'm putting you through. I know you hate me."

"Dad, I—"

"I wish I could die," his father continued, "and free you from your misery."

"I don't hate you, Dad. I don't want you to die," Josh said softly. But like Jessica, Sam Phearson could see straight through a lie. His eyes were open wounds and tears bled from them, trickling down his wrinkled cheeks. The room was suddenly too small for Josh, the walls closing in on him, and he had to flee. As he shut the door behind him, he heard his father choke on a sob.

———

The moon was a dead man's face grinning through the window blinds, casting striped shadows across the bed. Save for this alternating pattern of black and silver, darkness draped the room, and for that Josh was grateful, for the night hid his shame. "I'm sorry, Karla," he whispered, staring up at the ceiling, sheets that should have been stained with sweat instead laying cool against his skin.

"It's okay," his wife murmured. "It doesn't matter."

"Of course it matters."

"It happens, Josh. It's not the end of the world."

He felt rage rising like a dark tide, tried to suppress it, and failed. "What the hell's wrong with you?" he snapped. "I can't get it up, and you act like it's no big deal."

"Josh—"

"Don't you understand, Karla? I can't even make love to my own wife!"

"Keep your voice down," she said. "Jessica will hear you. Or your dad."

"Dad." He spat the word like an obscenity. "This is all his fault anyway."

She sat up, leaning on one elbow to face him. "What are you talking about?"

When she sat up, the sheet slipped down, baring her breasts. Josh savored her nakedness and tried to force his way to arousal, but nothing happened, not even so much as a twitch. "Dammit!" he exploded. "Can't you see, Karla? I'm getting old, just like my father!"

"That's ridiculous. You're only forty-seven. He's seventy-six."

"I can't explain it," Josh said. "It's like he's a mirror. When I look at him, I see myself, my future, and it scares the hell out of me. I don't want to be old and ugly. I don't want to buy stock in Depends because I crap my pants. And I sure as hell don't want to see a damn Viagra commercial on TV and think, 'Oh, yeah, hey, I need to refill my prescription so I can make love to my wife tonight.'"

"Josh, you're overreacting. I'm sure it was just a fluke."

He lay there in silence for several long moments, then said, "Karla, is it wrong to want your father to die?"

She looked at him, horrified. "How can you even think such a thing, Josh? He's your father."

"He's not the man he used to be, the one I loved."

"He's still your father. He always will be."

"I can't help it," he said softly. "I wish he would die."

Karla reached out to him, and he surrendered to her tender embrace. He anointed her skin with hot tears and hoped it help ease the chill she probably felt at his cold, merciless words. He sensed her lips moving in the dark, a silent prayer to a God he no longer acknowledged. He wondered what the prayer was.

Forgive him, Father, for he knows not what he says.

———

Sunlight streamed through the bathroom window, golden sparkles dancing off the mirror as Josh brushed his teeth and enjoyed the smooth glide of his tongue across plaqueless enamel. There was nothing quite like clean teeth.

He leaned over, spit into the sink, rinsed, stood up, looked in the mirror, and recoiled in horror. A choked cry strangled his throat, and he coughed, spraying spittle across the image in the glass. It was his image...

...but different. The reflection staring back at him was an eerie hybrid of him and his father. It was his face but torn

by the talons of time. His skin was furrowed, hanging from his skull in limp, sagging folds. His hair was streaked with white, brittle, the roots relinquishing their grip on his scalp. Drooping eyelids shrouded his cataracted pupils.

He stumbled back. "No. No, it can't be..." He took another step back, his calves bumping into the side of the tub, but his ancient image refused to retreat. Instead, it loomed closer, like a lover drawing near for a passionate kiss. He heard sibilant voices invading his head, haunting, whispering. You can run from the future, but the future never runs from you...you can run from the future...the future never runs...never...never...never ... *The chant became a howling chorus of insanity, shredding his mind with iron claws.*

"NO!" he shrieked, closing his eyes to barricade himself against the madness. He didn't know how long he held them shut, but when he opened them again, his reflection was a rotting ruin. His eyeballs burst open, and a river of maggots oozed from the blown sockets, squirming through diseased flesh and decaying bone. The worms writhed together, a collective mind unified by a common purpose. They merged and mated to emblazon a single, pulsing phrase across the bottom of the mirror like the caption of a painting: THE FUTURE

Josh screamed, "NOOOOO!!"

———

"—OO!!" Josh bolted up from his sweat-soaked pillow, the cry tearing from his throat, ripping through the dark silence.

Then he felt hands on him, touching, soothing,

comforting. "Shhhh," Karla murmured. "Easy, honey, it was just a nightmare, that's all."

Terror flooded through him, and fear-sweat formed a slick sheen on his skin. His blood felt like it had been replaced by ice. "No," he gasped, breath ragged, "it was real. Way too real."

She brushed her lips against his. "Relax. Go back to sleep."

"No." He pushed her away, threw back the covers, and began dressing.

She stared at him like he was losing his mind, and for all he knew, maybe he was. "Where are you going?" she asked. "Josh, it's four in the morning."

He slid into a jacket. "To church."

He saw the look of astonishment on her face. She couldn't have been more surprised if he had said he was going out to sacrifice a goat to Baal, smear the blood all over him, and dance naked in the moonlight while howling like a wolf. "But you hate church," she said. "You hate God, for that matter. What's changed?"

"Nothing's changed. I just hate my father more." He left, closing the door behind him, leaving her alone in the dark, no doubt wondering what the hell was wrong with her husband.

———

"The hour is early, my son."

"It may be too late for me, Father."

"Do you seek to confess?"

"No, Father."

"Have you no sins?"

"I don't really believe in sin."

"Then why have you come?"

"I'm frightened, Father."

"Of what?"

"I see things in the mirror."

"What kind of things?"

"Horrible things. Terrible things. Things that might be considered...unholy."

"Then why do you keep the mirror, my son?"

"What do you mean?"

"If what you see in the mirror strikes terror in your soul, then break the mirror and get rid of it."

"But...but I once loved the mirror. It was special to me."

"Love does not frighten. Love and fear are not companions. True love would rather be broken than horrify."

"So, I should break the mirror, Father?"

"Shatter it, my son."

————

The chilling chant scraped like iron nails across the blackboard of his mind.

Break the mirror...break the mirror...

It sent cold shudders slithering greasily down his spine, but there was no denying its power, the sweet allure of promise, the seductive call of freedom whispering just over the horizon.

Break the mirror...break the mirror...

Dawn crimsoned the sky like blood flowing into dark waters, the rays knifing through the bedroom window. Josh stood with his back to the light, face hidden in shadows. More darkness welled up from within him, the black obsession of his soul incarnating in his eyes.

Break the mirror...break the mirror...

He didn't really remember taking the Smith & Wesson .357 Magnum out of his nightstand, but there it was in his hand, sunbeams glinting off the stainless steel like flashes of fire. But the flame flashes did nothing to warm him. He still felt cold to his very marrow, as if his bones had been left to lie in an ice-caked crypt. He didn't know if he would ever feel warm again, but it didn't matter. All that mattered now was—

Break the mirror...break the mirror...

He cocked the hammer, his fevered mind transferring the chilling chant to his lips. "Break the mirror... break the mirror..." He raised the gun, feeling strangely detached, and took up the trigger slack.

His finger trembled, and in that heartbeat of hesitation, his dad's eyes opened. His father stared into the gaping mouth of the Magnum for a moment, then gazed beyond the gun and into the dead darkness of Josh's eyes. Josh felt the air crackle between them, as if the visual connection was a livewire, a line of raw communion between father and son.

He's not afraid. The revelation sliced into the flesh of Josh's subconscious like a million red-hot razors. *He doesn't hate me for what I'm about to do. Even now, looking into the eye of the Reaper, he loves me. He always has, he always will, even beyond the grave.*

But the subconscious does not rule the conscious, and Josh was committed to the play. Destiny's dice had been rolled, and as far as he was concerned, there was no calling them back.

Serenity graced his father's face. "Go on, son. Your mother's waiting for me on the other side, so go ahead and set yourself free from whatever it is that's troubling you."

Thunder roared in Josh's head, but in the hollow of his soul was nothing but grim silence. "I'm sorry, Dad," he murmured, knowing it was the final lie he would ever tell his father.

His father gave him a smile, then closed his eyes and folded his hands as if in prayer.

A single tear fell down Josh's cheek like a fallen dove. He closed his eyes—

"Forgive me, Father, for I have sinned."

—and pulled the trigger.

———

Karla bolted upright in bed, heart pounding, as two shots shattered the solitude of the dawn. From across the hall, she heard Jessica's terrified cry of "Mommy!"

Then she was running down the hall...flinging open her father-in-law's bedroom door...the images inside etching themselves into her retinas with the pain of a thousand sizzling tattoo needles...boring through her eyes...burning their horror forever into her mind.

All strength bled from her body, and she slumped to the floor in a boneless heap, a puppet with cut strings. She didn't even have the strength to scream, but could only whisper, "No...oh god please...no."

Josh was sprawled on the rug, gun barrel still in his mouth, smoke oozing from between his slack lips, the back of his head sprayed across the wall behind him.

Death spasms racked his body, as if his corpse suffered from rheumatism.

His father's head rested on a blood-sodden pillow, a single weeping hole in his forehead. Death had brought a peaceful smile to Sam Phearson's lips, erasing the ravages of time from his face, returning him to the handsome young man he had once been. Karla put a hand over her mouth and sobbed as she looked him, for it was like looking in a mirror and seeing her husband's face.

"Mommy?"

Oh, God. Karla turned toward Jessica, who stood in the doorway hugging a teddy bear, tears glistening on her cherubic cheeks. "You shouldn't be here, honey. Take Teddy and go back to bed."

"But Mommy, why does Daddy look so old?"

It was true. Death had made an old man out of Josh, sucking the youth and vitality from his features. His limbs still shook in rheumatic spasms. His muscle fibers were limp, like broken violin strings, and the flesh sagged on his bones. His own blood had back sprayed into his face, covering it with crimson wrinkles.

Before Karla could stop her, Jessica ran across the room and threw herself into her father's lifeless arms... sobbing...hugging...begging him to come back...wake up...tuck her into bed...kiss away her fears.

Karla's heart broke at the wrenching contrast of innocent youth and ancient death. She crawled across the floor, her own sobs echoing off the wall, and wrapped her arms around them both, the living and the dead...

...while Sam Phearson continued to smile peacefully.

THE PATRIOT

AUTHOR'S NOTE

While I have not included any in this collection, back in the '90s I wrote a lot of poetry focused on Vietnam veterans and how they were treated when they came back from the jungle kill-zones. This is the one piece of fiction I penned during that partic- ular phase, and it also touches on the subject of insanity, making it something of a companion to "Sanity's Twitch."

Ohmigod, they're burnin' the flag!

Why? *Why!* My arms move fast as I race my rickety ol' wheelchair around the edge of the crowd. Outta my way. Outta my way! I need to see! I see a—um, what are they called? Oh yeah, hippies—I see a hippy with slanted eyes. Maybe he's Korean. Or Chinese. Or Japanese. Don't matter. He's got sloped eyes, so I know he's a gook. You dirty scumbag. I spent two tours killin' your kind, and now you're here, burnin' our flag. *My* flag. He has set fire to the end of the flag. The flames are eating up the stripes. I smell the fire and think of hot jungles and burning villages. God, I miss the sweet smell of napalm.

The hippies are shouting. "Make love, not war!" they yell. "Peace, peace!" they scream. Don't you get it, you morons? Don't you understand? Peace comes in pieces. Pieces of skull. Pieces of brain. Pieces of flesh and bone. Pieces like the puzzle pieces the doc had me try to put together after my accident. I couldn't do it, but that's okay. Someone else can put that puzzle together. But nobody will ever be able to put the pieces of those soldiers back together. Those boys are like Humpty Dumpty, I guess.

The hippies have funny looks in their eyes as they yell and shout and watch the flag burn. It's the same look those VC sappers had in their slanty eyes when they snuck into our camps with bombs on their backs and blew the whole place to smithereens, themselves with it. Fanatics, we used to call 'em, but I don't know what that means anymore. I think it's 'cause of the accident, but I ain't sure. All I know is that I hate these people. Long-haired freaks! Idiots! You think you're fightin' for somethin', a cause? You don't know jack-all about fightin', you draft dodgin' cowards. You've never put your life on the line. Hell, you'd crap your pants the first time a bullet zipped past your ear. Bunch of slack-jawed sissies.

The flag's burnin' fast now. The cloth is turning black. It reminds me of burned flesh, and for a minute, I'm back in the POW camp. The hippies aren't hippies anymore. They're a squad of VC. My friend Jim—or is it Joe? I can't remember. Anyway, he's tied up, and the hippies, or gooks, or whatever, are burning him alive after shoving bamboo splinters under his fingernails. He's screaming. Oh god, I can smell his burnin' skin. C'mon, you fucking bastards! I'll kill ya! I'll kill ya all! I'll rip your goddamn guts right outta your dead bodies and wear 'em like a necklace. War is hell, but its jewelry can't be beat.

I'm back now. Back with the hippies. Smoke swirls through the air. The hippies notice me at last. They stare at me. What, you pissed that I'm here? Too bad. I don't care. Go ahead an' stare. Call me a baby killer. You weren't there. You don't know. You don't know crap. You're just a bunch of fools, all of ya, starin' at me like idiots. If I still had my legs, I'd kick all your asses, ya flag-burnin' bastards.

A girl, hair hangin' down to her tailbone, steps out of the crowd. She looks at my Army uniform, then throws something at me. "Baby killer!" she screams. The thing hits me in the head and falls to the ground. I look down. It's a plastic baby doll with a bullet hole in its head. Someone has used red paint to make it look like the doll's face is covered in blood.

I look at the girl and drool. It runs down my chin, nice and warm. I blow spit bubbles. The doc said I shouldn't do that, but it's so much fun. Almost as much fun as killin' the enemy.

The girl swears at me. Can't hear ya real well, babe, I'm too busy blowin' spit bubbles. She turns and walks away, looking over her shoulder at me like I'm dog crap. I'm not dog crap, bitch, you are. Flag-burnin' whore.

I raise my hand and touch where the doll hit my

head. There's a bump over the small round scar there. That's where the VC bullet hit me. Doc said it's the weirdest thing. Bullet went right through my brain and got stuck in my head but didn't kill me. I heard the doc talking to my sarge after I woke up and heard him say words like "mental retardation" and "simpleton." I don't think those are good words, but I'm not sure anymore. But that's not my fault. It's 'cause of the accident. I don't know why the doc keeps callin' it an accident, though, 'cause that gook SOB shot me on purpose. The doc says he don't know why I'm still alive. But I do. God saved me. Maybe I can pay Him back someday.

The flag is still burning. The hippies are singing now. Some stupid song about better days coming. Maybe it's the Beatles. I don't know, I don't remember, I don't care.

Now a man—no, wait, it's just a boy, must be a boy, 'cause his mustache is nothin' but peach fuzz—steps out of the crowd. "Yo, soldier boy!" he yells. "How's it feel to be a cripple? Murdering dirtbag! You deserve having your damn legs blown off!"

Screw you, asswipe! What you'll never know is that my legs got blown off when I stepped on a landmine while tryin' to save a young Vietnamese girl from a crossfire. Didn't do no good, she died anyway. Bullet in the heart. I don't know if it was an American bullet or VC. Doesn't matter. Dead is dead. Dead is forever. I may have lost my legs, but at least I have my life. Better than that poor girl.

The flag is ashes now. The hippies dance on it. They stomp on it with their sandals. I begin to cry. That flag is what I fought for, what my friends died for, what I lost my legs for, what I took a bullet in the head for. You scum, how dare you treat it like a dirty ol' rag. No respect, no loyalty. You're a bunch of traitors, all of ya! Dirty, gutless cowards! You don't know nothin' about red, white, and blue. Only color you know is yellow. I spin my chair around. I'm angry, but I'm glad I came. Old Glory, you had at least one friend to weep while you burned.

There are tears on my face. All I want to do is leave. But my way is blocked by one of the hippies. I look up at him. It's the gook, the one who set fire to the flag. His right hand is behind his back. "Outta my way," I growl.

The gook says nothing, just smiles.

"Outta my way," I growl again.

The gook takes his hand out from behind his back. His fingers are clenched tightly shut. He holds out his hand as if he wants to give me a present. His fingers slowly open, and the ashes of the flag fall down onto my lap. "America's blood is upon your soul, soldier," he says. "May you rot in Hell."

Rot in Hell? *Me?* I'll show you who's gonna rot in Hell! I'll kill you! I'll kill ya all! I'm a soldier. It's my duty. Get ready, ya flag-burnin', dope-smokin', draft-dodgin', VC-lovin' sons of bitches! Get ready to die! Die! DIE!

My hand comes up. Who put that gun there? Maybe it was God. I pull the trigger. The gook's face turns red. Ha! Ya like that, boy? Ya like that? Have some more. *Bang!* His brains fly out the back of his head in soggy clumps. I shoot again and again, and the enemy squad is bleeding and screaming and dropping, and my gun is empty, but I keep pulling the trigger because I am happy, so happy, and I am doing my duty. This is war, and I am a soldier. I'll kill 'em! I'll kill 'em all!

I hear the sirens. I see the lights. Who cares? They ain't really policemen, they're VC in disguise. I lift my gun. "For flag and freedom!" I scream. "Die, die, die!" I pull the trigger. Who cares if the gun's empty? It's the thought that counts.

And then there is pain. Lots of it. All over my body. And lots of holes, big ones. Blood pours out of the holes. Something slams into my head. My wheelchair tips backward, dumping me onto the ground. The pain is leaving now. Someone is standing over me. An enemy soldier. I can see his shiny badge. Now I can't see anything. There is blood in my eyes. But I can still hear. "Crazy vet," he says. Why is he speaking English? Gooks don't speak English. "If only you'd gotten your head blown off instead of your legs, would've been the best thing you could have done for this country."

I can't hear anymore.

Wait...I do hear something.

Flames.

Maybe another flag is burning.

THE DESECRATION

Desecrated sanctuary
Blackened souls in misty trances
Sacredness and evil married
See His head on silver lances

Black-robed rulers with tongues of oil
Poison words and menacing pens
Pay no heed their mortal coil
Seek thy pleasure in wicked dens

They have forsaken salvation
Yet still dare to eat God's flesh
Calling their souls to damnation
Forgetting the judgment savage

Desecraters of sacred blood
Beware the Reaper's icy grin
Ye spawned from remnants of the flood
Denied redemption for your sins

Desolate chapel burned to dust
Cleansing fire from Heaven rained
A righteous scourge so hot and just
From Hell's ashes begin again

THE RAZOR'S VOICE

AUTHOR'S NOTE

This is my most overtly religious story, with Christian symbolism so blatant, it barely qualifies as symbolism at all. While not deliberately designed so, nor written to be, I often consider this a companion piece to "Fallen Angel, Risen Dove." It originally started life as a poem but then morphed into prose, and if we're being honest, the final result resembles some avant-garde merging of the two—a hybrid that is neither poetry nor story but something created from the DNA of both mediums.

I see my face in the crimsoned mirror of the dripping razor blade. My haunted eyes stare back at me, every secret of hell lurking within the hollow, sunken sockets. Dilated pupils expand with each heartbeat as heroin rides through my veins on red liquid horses. The twin diamonds of my enlarged pupils are azure-hued and embedded in a sea of blood-stained snow, tiny veins violating the virgin sanctity of the whites.

Staring at my razored reflection, I see the scarlet web spread across my optic tissue, edging toward my irises. What happens when those thin red strands finally trap my blue orbs? Will they continue dilating, expanding until they can expand no more, finally bursting like overloaded water sacks? I envision my eyes exploding like pulpy grapes, flecks of sky-blue tissue mixing with less vivid gouts of vitreous jelly. My life pours out through my blasted sockets, and I weep, a cascade of blood and tears, pain and ecstasy. Heaven gleams in the distance, but Hell is just a breath away. Angels call, but devils answer, my soul the prize in this holy war.

Pain suddenly flares in my wrists, reminding me of what I have done, and the visions fade like fog before a blazing sun. The razor is still before my eyes, my blood still drips from the blade, but death is sluggish, as if the Reaper is shackled by a ball and chain, struggling to reach me but being cheated by a greater force. I crave that icy, bony kiss...please, dear God, don't deny me.

I feel no horror at praying to die. *Life* is horror. I doubt God can hurt me more in death than He has while I draw breath. My life is a living hell, God seemingly as cruel as Satan. Is my belief not enough, my faith so fragile that He must torment me until a razor's kiss is my only salvation?

My metallic reflection blurs as my hands start to shake, but not before I've seen the dark circles wreathing my eyes like Saturn's rings. The razor falls into the sink and clatters against the white porcelain, staining it red. I can't stand to look at myself anymore; can't stand to see the damned, wasted husk I have become. How can a man look himself in the eye as he takes his own life? I am no fool. I know there is no nobility in suicide. It is a desperate act, a creation of hell. It is what remains when a man has been stripped of everything, when the thorns of life have shredded through his flesh and ripped out his heart. Suicide is the act of a man who has seen God in the devil's mirror.

Why can't I die? Please, God, if You have even an ounce of mercy, hear me now. You made this life unbearable. At least have the kindness to grant me the release I crave.

The razor whispers to me from the bottom of the sink.

Kiss me again...feel me...taste me...let me caress your flesh...

I reach down and grasp the ivory handle. I stare at the weapon for a long moment.

Don't hesitate...do it...another kiss and eternity will be yours...freedom...release...just one more kiss away...

In sudden fury, I slash again, wound upon wounds, cutting deeper until steel rasps against bone. My wrists gape wide, chasms of agony. I fall to my knees, the proper pose for a supplicant sinner. The thin red veins invading my eyes finally reach my pupils. I throw my head back as visions explode through my mind...

The sky rages over a barren wasteland. Lightning rips across the bellies of black clouds, and rain spills from the jagged wounds, whipped across the land by lashing winds. In the storm, two figures—one in black, one in white—battle. Silhouetted behind them, a wooden cross enveloped in a skull-shaped shadow. At the base of the cross, a third figure, a man with blood-shot blue diamonds for eyes. The stained orbs glisten in the darkness with desperate intensity, and I realize the man is me. Lightning sears the dark again. I see my opened wrists and the gaping hole in my chest where my heart used to be.

Demons skitter and scamper and frolic in the sodden darkness, guttural voices urging the man in black on to victory. The dark-cloaked figure is armed with a massive hammer and three rusty spikes. The man in white is unarmed, but the demonic chants are contagious. I scream for the man in black, feeling only hate for the underdog.

Thunder roars. Lightning flashes. Rain falls. The man in white battles weakly, if he battles at all, and is forced backward until he is pressed against the rugged cross. Almost of their own volition, his arms spread wide in crucifix fashion. His face is resigned as the demons cheer and the hammer falls. The loud crack of steel-on-steel mates with a crack of thunder, and the noise shatters the earth. Rocks split. Fissures jag across the ground like varicose veins. A rending cry fills the world with the terrible sound of angels being ravaged.

The spike impales the man's wrist, punching through the bones, nailing him to the cross. Blood spurts from torn flesh, spraying across my face. Red rivulets run down my body, cloaking me in crimson, as agony and ecstasy wage war within me. I fall to my knees at the foot of the cross, the crucified man's blood flowing into my wounds. Sweet fire burns away the pain...

The pain in my wrists ebbs. The vision vanishes. I am back on my bathroom floor, the razor beside me, death imminent. The floor around me is wet with blood and my wrists...

My god...my...my wrists...

My wrists are sealed.

The flesh is unmarred, save for a single cross-shaped scar. I blink, but this is no vision. When I look again, the cross is still there, etched into my skin like a brand.

I pick up the razor and listen.

I can't hear its voice anymore.

GOLGOTHA'S WINE

AUTHOR'S NOTE

*"Golgotha's Wine" started out as an experiment—
could I write a story using nothing but dialogue? So,
I set the tale in a confessional, where a priest listens
to the strangest confession in the history of mankind
and discovers that even evil likes sweet things...blood
sweet, that is.*

"Go ahead, my son."

"Bless me, Father, for I have sinned."

"How long since your last confession?"

"I have never confessed."

"Then this visit is long overdue. Confess everything, and you will be forgiven."

"But you do not even know what I am."

"Of course I do. You're someone in need of forgiveness, just like every other human being."

"No, Father, I am...something else."

"I don't believe you. Listen, if all you're going to do is waste my time with this nonsense, then—"

"If I am just a man, Father, a mere mortal, how is it then that I have knowledge of your secret sins?"

"What the—I don't have any secret sins!"

"So, the Church no longer frowns on priests who engage in homosexual acts with male prostitutes?"

"What...how did...I don't know what you're talking about."

"Relax, Father, your sins are safe with me. I only mention them to prove I am not human."

"Then what are you?"

"Something caught between worlds. Something with one foot in Heaven and the other in Hell."

"That's impossible."

"No, Father, it is not."

"You mentioned Hell...does that mean you believe in the devil?"

"Of course. He is my father."

"What about God? You believe in Him too?"

"Can there be one without the other?"

"Do you believe He's alive?"

"I know He is. I cannot drink the blood of the dead."

"Why on earth would you drink blood at all?"

"I have no choice. I am *nosferatu*."

"*What?*"

"A vampire, Father."

"Now you're talking crazy. There's no such thing as—"

"Your disbelief does not change the truth."

"But...but this is a *church*, a holy place. Why would a vampire come here? What are you looking for?"

"Redemption. Salvation. Absolution."

"For what? What's your sin?"

"I drank the blood of Christ."

"Oh my god!"

"Precisely. Put down the crucifix, Father, it makes me nervous."

"How did you know I—"

"I have a sixth sense for crosses, stakes, and holy water."

"Oh, yeah. Right. Of course. So anyway...when did you drink Christ's blood?"

"At Golgotha, the scene of the crucifixion."

"Thought you didn't like crosses."

"Think about it, Father. Before Christ's death, crosses were nothing more than instruments of execution. The cross did not become a sacred symbol—and thus a danger to the *nosferatu*—until *after* the crucifixion."

"I guess that makes sense, but I still don't understand why you drank His blood."

"To test His divinity. As I said, I cannot drink the blood of the dead. It is like poison to me. So, if Christ was actually the Son of God, then He was not really dead on the cross and tasting His blood would not harm me. And it didn't. Truth be told, I have never felt so alive as when that sweet blood ran down my throat."

"I...I don't know what to say."

"Say I am forgiven. Give me absolution."

"I can't!"

"Why not?"

"Don't you get it? Don't you realize what you did? You sucked the Savior's blood!"

"Do you grasp the irony of which you speak, Father?

You are telling me I am *damned* because I drank the blood of *God*."

"I'm done talking to you. Get out of here."

"Not without absolution."

"You can't have it! You can never have it! You're a creature of Hell!"

"Is not God the creator of all things?"

"Shut up! *Just shut your mouth!* You border on blasphemy!"

"I border on truth, Father. You just refuse to accept it."

"Just because God created you doesn't automatically make you one of His children. God also created the devil and the demons."

"I am neither."

"You cringe at crosses."

"I know of evil *men* who wince at the sight of a cross, yet redemption is not denied *them*, should they seek it."

"You drink blood!"

"Are there murderers in Heaven, Father?"

"That's different! They're *human!*"

"No difference. Absolve me."

"GO TO HELL! You hear me? You go straight back to the Hell you came from!! Hey...what...what are you... wait a minute...you can't come in here...get out...stay away from me..."

"I'm thirsty, Father."

"Oh no, please don't do this! Oh, please, God, no, I'm begging you!"

"Salvation is found in the blood, Father."

"No please don't OH SWEET GOD IN HEAVEN NO IT HURTS OH GOD IT HURTS!!!"

"Your blood is sweet, Father, like wine. Only Christ's was sweeter."

"Stop...please...the pain..."

"Pray you are wrong, Father. Pray there is salvation for my kind, for you are now one of us."

"No..."

"yes, Father. As the scriptures say, 'Old things are passed away; behold, all things are become new.'"

"You...goddamned..."

"Perhaps, Father. Perhaps."

AN HONEST MISTAKE

AUTHOR'S NOTE

They say every horror author has to write at least one werewolf story and one vampire story. Well, this is my vampire story. It was written way back in 2001 and was originally intended to kickstart a series about a Vatican-sponsored team of vamp killers. The series hasn't happened yet, probably because when vampires started to sparkle, I lost interest in them.

It was a good day to kill a vampire.

That was the thought flitting through Jack Stone's mind as he strolled down the heat-shimmered sidewalk of Miami. His partner, a Black man named Lucas, walked beside him, and up ahead about a block was their destination, The Crystal Tower, a luxurious high-rise hotel glittering like a stack of mirrors, catching and reflecting the hot Florida sun so that the building looked like it was exploding with rainbows. It was a sight engineered to catch the eye, and that's exactly what it did. But it couldn't distract Stone's focus from the task at hand, and that was slaughtering a suckhead.

They passed two priests walking in the opposite direction, the salty breeze from the nearby ocean ruffling their hair. Stone figured they were not the last men of the cloth he and Lucas would encounter. There was some big Catholic convention in town this week-end, a gathering of cardinals, bishops, and assorted upper-echelon priests. In fact, during their briefing for this hit, Stone and Lucas had been informed by their handler, an enigmatic priest known only as Father Thomas, that a large contingent of cardinals was staying at The Crystal Tower. Stone got a kick out of the thought of priests and vampires sleeping next to each other. The pope would blow a gasket if he knew.

The two priests nodded in greeting as they passed. Their white collars gleamed bone-bright in the harsh sunlight, and Stone could only imagine how hot it was in those black penguin suits. Poor bastards had to be sweating their balls off. Then again, being priests, they probably didn't have much use for their balls anyway. Stone wondered what the priests would think if they knew he and Lucas also worked for the Church. Some-how, he doubted these guys had any knowledge of the covert Sacred Order of Blood. Not many outside the pope's innermost circle did.

"Hey, Lucas," Stone said. The light windbreaker he wore was out of place in this heat, but it was the only way he could conceal the Ingram MAC-10 submachine gun slung around his neck. "Think you'll ever get tired of running around the world butchering blood-suckers?"

Lucas shrugged his big, broad shoulders, and the backpack he wore made a rattling sound, just like a sack of wooden stakes would be expected to. "Don't know," he replied. "Haven't given it much thought. You?"

"Hell, no. I love this life. Sometimes I think killing vamps is better than sex."

Lucas grinned, teeth flashing white in the ebony of his face. "You must be having some pretty lousy sex then."

"Hell of a thing to say about your mother," Stone retorted.

As they continued toward The Crystal Tower, Stone reflected on the chain of events that had brought them to this place and time. Hard to believe they had been slayers for five years now. The old cliché was true. Time really does fly when you're having fun.

It all began with an unholy scandal in the Vatican, that bastion of purity, righteousness, and rampant hypocrisy. Stone had never heard the real story, but from what he pieced together from all the rumors, about a dozen or so years ago, the pope had decided the whole sexual abstinence thing wasn't his bag and had begun putting his sacred scepter into a nun's holiest of holies.

Unfortunately, the cherry-popping pope had failed to commit the cardinal sin of wearing a condom. The nun got knocked up, and the pope found himself with a bastard son. It was testament to the Church's massive influence and scope of power that they had been able to conceal the whole scandal without a single media leak.

Of course, rumor was, the cover up began with the "disappearance" of the slutty nun, but that was one rumor Stone had a tough time swallowing. Getting laid was one thing—even the pope had urges, for god's sake—but murder was a whole other ball game.

"Hey, Lucas," Stone said, "you ever buy that bullshit about the big guy having the mother of his child whacked?"

Lucas shrugged. "I suppose it's possible. They say the guy's crazy, you know."

"Yeah, but that didn't happen until the vamps got his kid."

The pope's son had been six years old when he vanished. His body was found three days later, as dead as dead can be, nearly every inch of his flesh covered with punctures and not a single drop of blood left in his mangled veins. The authorities chalked it up to an anti-Catholic ritualistic murder, but the pope, though he would never admit it in public, believed vampires had taken his son's life, had fed upon his sweet, innocent blood. He declared a holy war against "the blood-sucking demons from Hell," and thus was born the Sacred Order of Blood, the Church's super-secret kill squad whose sole purpose was to hunt down and exterminate vampires. Unlike other Orders, the Sacred Order of Blood was not comprised of men of peace, but men of war. Belief in God and faith in Christ were valued far less than the ability to kill without compunction.

At the time he had been approached to join the Order, Stone had been eking out a living on the mean streets of Chicago, running low-level hits for the local mob bosses. The Church had promised him absolution for his sins as well as obscene amounts of money if he would lay down his guns (figuratively speaking) and pick up a wooden stake. Stone hadn't bothered telling them the money meant a hell of a lot more to him than absolution; he'd simply said, "Hell, yeah." That had been five years ago, and the killing since then had been ceaseless. Stone had long ago lost count of how many bloodsuckers he had sent to Hell.

Lucas and Stone reached the entrance to The Crystal Tower, passing several more priests along the way. The pneumatic doors hissed open at their approach, the sound reminding Stone of the final gasp of a dying vampire, usually in the last second before Lucas lopped off its head and silenced it forever. Inside, the lobby absolutely reeked of grandeur, from the marbled floor to the diamond-studded chandeliers dangling from the cathedral ceiling to the gently burbling fountain in the center. The place shrieked wealth, and Stone, hardly a philanthropist at heart, still couldn't help but ponder the fact that church officials were here, sleeping on $750-a-night beds, while children starved to death in third world countries. Stone's knowledge of scripture was sketchy, but he was pretty sure Christ hadn't spent much time between silk sheets.

Lucas looked decidedly unimpressed as he gazed around the lobby, taking it all in. "Ostentatious," he said. Stone wanted to slap him. Lucas had an annoying habit of using at least one big word a day, and it drove Stone nuts. The guy must sleep with a goddamn thesaurus under his pillow.

Stone headed toward the elevators. "If you're done spouting off like some kind of walking rectum," he said over his shoulder, "what do you say we go ram a stake up some vampire's ass?"

"Right behind you, pal."

They made their way through the crowd of elitist, high-society snobs who apparently had nothing better to do with their day than stand around the fountain and feign importance. With their stubbled faces and low-key clothes, Stone and Lucas looked out of place among the Armani suits and $10,000 Rolexes, and they drew numerous glances of disgust. But the instant Stone turned his cold, hard eyes on whoever happened to be sneering at them at the given moment, the look of disgust changed to fear, and the person immediately averted his gaze. *That's right*, Stone thought grimly, *don't even think about messing with me.*

The people waiting in front of the elevators parted as they approached, giving them a wide berth. It was as if they could actually smell the violence on them. A bell dinged, the elevator doors slid open, and the two vampire killers entered. Nobody else even tried to get on with them. "You got the room number?" Stone asked.

Lucas pulled a piece of paper out of his pocket and looked at it. "Room sixty-six."

Stone punched the button for the sixth floor, and the doors slid shut. The car was spacious enough, he supposed, but its stainless-steel walls and claustrophobic closeness reminded him of a coffin, which in turn made him vaguely uneasy. Maybe he had been at this business too long. Sometimes it seemed like he saw fangs, crucifixes, and sarcophagi wherever he went.

He checked his weapon on the ride up, making sure the magazine was seated properly, that there was a bullet in the chamber, and that the sound-suppressor was firmly attached to the threaded muzzle. In vamp-hunting vernacular, Stone was known as a "stopper." It was his job to keep the vampire incapacitated long enough for Lucas, the "staker," to move in and finish off the fucker. Bullets didn't kill a bloodsucker, but they damn sure slowed it down, and Stone had selected the MAC-10 for strictly that reason. With its hellishly fast cyclic rate, the blocky assault weapon emptied a thirty-two-round clip loaded with 9mm slugs in less than 1.5 seconds. Even the biggest, baddest bloodsucker went down beneath that barrage, allowing Lucas to go to work with the stake and machete and put the mother-fucker out of its misery. It was a well-designed system that usually worked flawlessly, but like all systems, sometimes an unforeseen monkey wrench mucked things up. Just last week they had run into a vampire wearing a bulletproof Kevlar vest. Now *that* had been a real bitch.

Now it was another hotel, another assignment, another vampire ready for its second death—this one more permanent, hopefully.

The elevator slid noiselessly to a halt, and the doors opened into a hallway every bit as elegant as the lobby downstairs. Stepping out of the elevator, Stone's boots sank into carpeting so plush it was like walking on smoke.

There was nobody in the hall, and they found Room 66 in a matter of seconds. Stone slipped the MAC-10 from under his coat and thumbed off the safety. It made a sharp little click, a sound Stone found strangely soothing.

Lucas looked at him. "You ready?"

Stone's finger curled around the curve of the trigger. It felt cold and metallic. It felt *good*. "Oh, yeah," he said, adrenaline surging through his veins. "Let's do it." This was what he lived for, the rush of combat, the high of carnage, the narcotic of killing.

Lucas kicked in the door, putting all his considerable weight behind the blow, and it flew open. The hinges screeched under the strain of holding the door to the jamb. Stone charged into the room, bloodlust burning up his veins. It was dark in here, as expected—contrary to popular myth, vampires can survive sunlight, but it causes them a lot of pain, and they start to smoke like a pack of Camels—and Stone couldn't see jackshit, just shadows. But he saw a figure rising from the bed, and that was good enough for him.

"Die, you son of a bitch!" he snarled, and the MAC-10 leaped in his hands, flame spitting from the suppressor as the bullets tore across the room and into the thing on the bed. Due to the suppressor, the sound of the shots was very quiet, but the heavy *thwack-thwack-thwack* of hot lead ripping into meat and bone was anything but. The sound was wet and loud and echoed off the now-blood-spattered walls of the room, and Stone loved every second of it.

The thing didn't make a sound, which surprised Stone—usually the suckers howled and moaned and made all sorts of commotion before being dispatched. But this one just flopped backward on the bed and laid still. "Nail the son of a bitch, Lucas," Stone rasped.

For such a big man, Lucas moved with surprising speed and a sort of lethal grace. He rushed over to the bed, pulled a huge stake—eighteen inches of silver-tipped oak—out of his bag of tricks and drove it right through the bastard's chest. Stone felt damn near orgasmic as he heard the wonderful sound of cracking sternum and saw a crimson volcano geyser into the air as the stake punched into the thing's heart. God, he loved this job!

Lucas twisted the stake viciously and more blood billowed into the air. Stone could see that Lucas's arms were covered in a thick red rain. He also saw Lucas recoil as if the blood shocked him, but that didn't make any sense. Over the years, Lucas had been drenched in enough plasma to fill the Red Sea. He was immune to the feelings of disgust the average person might experience when splattered with someone's arterial fluids.

"What's the matter?" Stone asked. "Finish it off."

"It's warm," Lucas said, not moving. The stake jutted from the dead thing's chest like some sort of obscene growth, a tumor of the most terminal kind.

"What are you babbling about?" Stone growled.

"It's warm!" Lucas said again, a shrillness creeping into his voice. "The blood! It's fucking warm!"

Stone's enthusiasm withered like a week-old rose. "Shit!" he hissed. Vampire blood was cold. *Very* cold. Cold like an ice-soaked crypt carved into the center of an ancient glacier. The last thing Lucas should have been feeling was warmth.

"Hit the lights," Lucas said.

Stone fumbled along the wall until his fingers found the switch. He hesitated for a moment, part of him—hell, *most* of him—not wanting to face the truth, dreading what he would see when the lights came on, but he also saw no reason to delay the inevitable. He flicked the switch.

155

Neither of them spoke for a long moment. It was Lucas who finally broke the silence. "We are so fucked."

Yeah, that about sums it up, Stone thought. The thing on the bed was dead, all right, no doubt about that. But it wasn't a vampire. Stone took one look at the black clothes and white, blood-spattered clerical collar and realized Lucas's statement did not begin to do justice to the situation. Mere words could not begin to describe how fucked they were.

Lucas, for some stupid reason, felt the need to state the obvious. "We killed a priest, man." For the first time in their five years of working together, Stone heard an edge of panic in Lucas's voice. He couldn't blame him. Assigned to slay vampires, they had instead slain one of the Church's own, and Stone seriously doubted all the apologizing, genuflecting, and ring-kissing in the world would save them from this bloody mess.

Without really thinking about it, Stone ejected the spent magazine and fed a fresh one into the MAC-10. Smoke still trickled from the suppressor, twisting languidly toward the ceiling. Stone watched it rise and wished he felt that relaxed. "They can't blame us," he said, trying to convince himself as much as Lucas. "We were just operating on the information Father Thomas gave us."

"They're the Roman goddamned Catholic Church," Lucas replied sourly. "They can do any damn thing they please, including calling down the wrath of God to Sodom and Gomorrah our asses."

Stone abruptly had an image of he and Lucas bent over the Throne while the Almighty rammed thunderbolts up their backsides. It wasn't an image designed to soothe the nerves, but it did wonders for the pucker effect. "It's not the wrath of God I'm worried about," he said. "It's the wrath of Father Thomas. That guy can snap his fingers, and our asses will be run through the meat grinder. You ever seen butt burger? Not a pretty sight."

"Are you kidding me?" Lucas said. "We killed a man of God, and you're not worried that the Big Guy's gonna be pissed?"

"Plenty of people want a piece of me," Stone replied. "God can wait His fucking turn. Besides, we're operating under a cloak of absolution, remember?"

"I don't think this is what the Church meant when they said all our sins would be absolved," Lucas said. "Besides, this fuckup is our fault—well, mine anyway—not theirs."

Stone jacked the bolt, injecting a round into the chamber. "What are you talking about? We were just using the info they gave us. Not our fault they got the room number wrong."

"They didn't," Lucas said. "I read it upside down."

"Huh?"

Lucas pulled the piece of paper with the room number on it from his pocket and handed it to Stone. "What's that say?"

Stone looked at it. "Sixty-six, just like you said."

"Yeah, that's what I said," Lucas replied. "Problem is the room we wanted to hit is *ninety-nine*. Get it? I read the friggin' paper upside down and thought it was sixty-six."

Stone had to resist the sudden urge to put a couple of rounds between his partner's eyes. He gritted his teeth and said, "Honest mistake." What a fucking pooch-screw this had turned out to be, and all because the number nine looked like six when turned upside down. They were in a world of hurt all because of some freak chance of mathematics. Who said God didn't have a sadistic sense of humor?

There had to be a way out of this mess. There always was. Stone firmly believed that whenever one door slammed shut in your face, another one opened. Even in your darkest hour, there was always a glimmer of light if you looked hard enough. It was just a matter of finding that thin thread of hope. As his mind sifted through possibilities, desperately seeking a solution to this clusterfuck, he walked over to the corpse.

After years of killing vampires, whose flesh regenerated after being struck by bullets, Stone had forgotten just how much damage a volley of high-velocity hornets could do to a human body. Hit by every 9mm mangler in Stone's magazine, the priest had practically been turned inside out. It wasn't a pretty sight. The holy man had taken a whole lot of killing. But at least it had been quick, thank God for small favors. Maybe he and Lucas could get a reduced sentence in Hell. Stone figured he could stand frying for a few millennia as long as he knew there was a respite at the end. It was the thought of slow sizzling on Satan's spit for all eternity with no possibility of parole that didn't sit so well with him.

"What do you want to do?" Lucas asked. The blood spatters on his forearms looked like red polka dots.

The seed of an idea formed in Stone's head, blossoming slowly, like a wildflower after a heavy rain. Sure, it was as half-assed as a bisected donkey, but at this point it was the best he could come up with. "Give me the machete," he said.

Lucas didn't argue, content to let Stone make any and all decisions. He reached into his sack, pulled out the short, heavy-bladed machete, and handed it to Stone.

"Step back," Stone said. Lucas complied, retreating from the blood-soaked bed. Stone moved into position, laying the thick blade against the priest's throat, sizing up the blow.

"You mind telling me just what the hell you're doing?" Lucas asked from behind him.

"Getting our butts out of the sling you put them in." Stone raised the machete and brought it down in one smooth, powerful arc. The blade cut cleanly through flesh and cartilage, neatly splitting the priest's Adam's apple, but then got stuck in the vertebrae at the back of the neck. "You've got to be kidding me," Stone muttered. He felt like a frigging rookie. It had been years since he'd failed to take a head off with one blow. The blade was stuck good, too. He had to yank hard to dislodge it. But it finally came free ,and a second chop finished the job, accompanied by the loud, wet crack of separating bone. The severed head rolled away from the neck stalk as if repulsed by the raw red flesh and knob of butchered spine.

Stone reached over and picked it up by the hair. It was heavy, like a lumpy pumpkin, but getting lighter by the second as blood dribbled out of it. The eyes were the worst. They were wide open, staring at him, through him, into whatever eternity waited beyond the business end of a bullet. The death stare didn't bother him, but it was just disgraceful to die with your eyes open. He would rather die with his dick hanging out than die with his eyes open like that. It was just *wrong*.

159

Blood continued to drip. "Get the bag," Stone said to Lucas.

Lucas took a plastic garbage bag out of his sack and brought it over to the bed, holding it open so Stone could drop the head inside. Loaded with dead weight, the bag drooped almost to the floor. Lucas tied it off and dropped it back into the sack. "Now what?"

"Now we haul ass out of here, file down the priest's teeth, and go collect our money."

Lucas looked at him as if he had said they were going ice-fishing in Hawaii. "Are you out of your damn mind, man?"

"Think about it," Stone said. "It's perfect. Not only do we get ourselves out of this jam—a jam *you* put us in, I might add—but we get to collect our fee as well. Father Thomas isn't going to know the difference between a vampire head and a human head with pointy teeth. I doubt *we* could tell the difference. He'll just fork over the money, and no one will be the wiser."

"You're crazy."

Stone could tell by his partner's tone of voice he was almost convinced. "*I'm* crazy?" Stone echoed. "Let me tell you what crazy would be. Crazy would be reporting back to Father Thomas and telling him we killed a priest because you read the room number upside down. Compared to that option, my plan is the epitome of sanity."

Lucas still hesitated. Stone let the silence draw out, giving his partner time to mull things over. It was so quiet Stone imagined he could actually hear the sound of all the blood congealing. But the wait paid off, because Lucas finally said, "Okay, let's do it."

"Now you're talking," Stone said. He slung the

MAC-10 around his neck and pulled his windbreaker tight around him to conceal it. "Let's get out of here."

They exited the room, leaving the smell of blood and the lingering scent of panic behind them. They rode the elevator down to the bottom floor, wove their way through the crowd of wealth in the ostentatious lobby, and out onto the hot Miami street. The heat instantly rose up around them like wraiths, clutching at their skin with invisible fingers, trying to suck the moisture from their bodies. Around them, pedestrians passed by, oblivious to the grisly cargo in Lucas's sack. Stone started to relax, a grin spreading across his face. They had gotten away with it. They had failed to complete their mission, murdered a priest, and covered up their mistake with an atrocity, but they were going to walk away unscathed. Father Thomas would be none the wiser, and God was apparently a non-factor today.

"What the hell are you grinning about?" Lucas demanded.

Stone clapped his partner on the back. "Let's go give Father Thomas some head."

"You're a sick, sick man, Stone."

Stone laughed aloud, raising his face to the sun.

He never saw the taxicab that suddenly swerved out of traffic, jumped the curb, and mowed them down until it was too late. He would never hear the driver's statement to police, corroborated by testimony from the passenger, that the steering wheel had just suddenly wrenched to the left. "It was as if the car was possessed," the shaken cabbie told the cops. He would never know that an inspection of the taxicab revealed the vehicle to be in sound condition with no faulty mechanics of any kind.

All Stone knew as he lay in a crushed, mangled heap, the last seconds of his life running out of him in thick red rivers, heart and lungs shish-kabobbed by shards of shattered sternum and broken ribs, was that the sack containing the priest's head was lying right in front of his eyes.

And he could have sworn he heard someone laughing in there.

FALLEN ANGEL, RISEN DOVE

AUTHOR'S NOTE

I honestly don't remember exactly what was going through my head or what catalyst propelled me when I penned "Fallen Angel, Risen Dove." In many ways, it is the darkest and bleakest of my stories in this collection. It's not the most violent tale by any stretch of the imagination, but it brims with an ashen aura of hopelessness. Because some people will willingly walk through Hell in the hope of finding love. But if there is hope in Hell, then you can bet your ass it comes with a whopper of a price tag because the devil gives no bargains.

MARK ALLEN

ACT I

Dear Diary,

Midnight has passed like the summer shower that swept through earlier, casting its offering of rain on the land. Moonlight shimmers on the wet grass, and it seems as if the meadow is strewn with diamonds. I pen these words by candle flame, sitting under the old oak I've called friend ever since I can remember, in whose boughs I played in a time more innocent than now. A time before Dad caused my tears and pain. The tears come from the agony within, the pain from the agony without, the wounds Mom inflicted upon my flesh when I told her what I am about to tell you. But it's not her fault. The booze made her beat me.

Dad came again last night, just as he has once a week for the past three years, ever since I turned fourteen. I feign sleep, heart thudding with dread as clothing rustles, the sound of Dad disrobing. I squeeze my eyes shut lest I see his shadow on the wall, his pulsing desire growing like a ravenous alien beast. Dear God, why must it be this way? Why is this the only sign of my father's affection? Why can't he love me like other fathers, with simple words, a pat on the head, a kiss on the cheek?

When the nocturnal visits first began, I whimpered at the touch of his hands on my skin, sliding in an unfatherly way over my young body. But he cured my cries with the back of his hand, and I learned to suffer in silence.

But silent suffering is not eternal, dear Diary. It must end somehow, somewhere. Last night was the end

*of my silence, for though I begged him to wait until my
time had passed, he took me anyway. My God, what
kind of father doesn't care if he sires an incestuous
bastard? Are You listening, God? Can You hear me?*

The pen fell from Angel Rathmore's trembling fingers.
Tears blotted the diary page, smearing the ink into
black swirls as she answered her own questions. No,
God wasn't listening. No, He couldn't hear her. For if
He could, He wouldn't let a father vent his twisted
lust on his teenage daughter's body. And Angel
refused to believe there was *no* God. For without God,
there was no hope. At least belief in God offered a
glimmer of salvation, even if He was deaf to her
anguished cries.

Just like her mother.

She had approached her mother this morning after
vomiting into the water-stained toilet. As she pushed
the handle and watched the mess swirl away, she
wished it was that easy to flush away the memories she
knew would haunt her to the grave.

She came downstairs slowly, listening for any sign
of Dad, but apparently, he had already gone to work.
Wonder if he talks about me, she thought. *Does he go into
the breakroom and say, "Hey, boys, banged my daughter
last night. Lemme tell ya, she is one sweeeeet piece of ass."*

Angel paused on the last stair, fighting tears. She
preferred to cry at night, alone, just herself and the
shadows. She heard the sound of Mom slamming a
bottle down on the table in the kitchen. *Please, God,*
Angel prayed, *let her be sober. I need her to soothe me, hold
me, tell me she loves me even if Daddy doesn't. God, please, I
can't live without love anymore.*

Armed with a prayer, she entered the kitchen. "Mom, can I talk to you?"

She instantly realized God must still be deaf because her mother was already drunk, six empty beer bottles lined up before her in a haphazard line. She had graduated to whiskey, the bottle of Jack Daniels in her hand half gone.

Drusilla Rathmore turned bleary eyes on her own child. "Whuh?" she grunted, then swigged from the bottle, guzzling greedily as the liquor poured down her throat.

Angel didn't know whether to cry or scream. "Jeez, Mom, it's not even ten o'clock yet."

"Mind yer own bishness, Anshel."

"But I needed to talk to you."

"Sho talk."

Angel glared at the ugly bottles that had reduced her mother to a wasted shell. They were like little brown demons that invaded her body, sucked out her soul, and left behind this pitiful husk. This Bud's for you? More like this *hell's* for you.

Angel reached out and touched her mom's hand, the one wrapped around the whiskey bottle. "Mom, there's something I need to tell—"

Her mother jerked her arm away. "Doan toush my whishky," she slurred sloppily. "Leave me 'lone."

Frustrated, Angel wanted to hurt her mother for hurting her. She lashed out with her only weapon—the brutal truth. "Mom, Dad's been raping me."

A silence followed her announcement, so still that it amplified the tiniest sound to jet-roar intensity. The clock on the wall tick-tocked with a noise like a drag-on's footsteps. The refrigerator's hum screamed like a hundred banshees. The warm air blowing from the baseboard heating vents howled like a whirlwind.

A whirlwind also brewed in her mom's eyes. Angel saw it coming, rising from the sodden depths of her mother's mind with explosive fury. Drusilla Rathmore lurched to her feet and shattered the surrealistic silence with an angry roar. "Liar!" No more slur. "You lying little whore!"

"Mom, no—"

Her mother's hand whipped out and cracked across Angel's face. Pain burned through her cheek. "Don't you *dare* talk about your father that way," Drusilla hissed.

"But it's true! It's been happening since I was fourteen!"

"Liar!" Her mother busted the whiskey bottle against the edge of the table, leaving her clenching only the long neck with a few jagged shards jutting from it. "You lying little slut, I'll kill you!"

"Mom, please—"

The broken bottle flicked out.

Angel staggered back, forearm gashed and bleeding. The wound gaped raw and pink for a moment, and then the blood surfaced with a spurt and spattered on the linoleum floor.

"Bitch!" her mother screamed. "Lying whore!" She grabbed a beer bottle and flung it at her daughter, catching her on the shoulder. The other bottles followed.

As Angel felt the bottles bruising her body, she realized there was no love to be found in this home...if a house without love could even be called a home. She fled from the kitchen, sobbing, chased by flying bottles and the shrieking curses of her mother. It was the last time she would ever set foot in that room...

> *...for I've decided to run away, dear Diary. I can't live here anymore. I can't live without love, so I'll go in search of it. I know somewhere out there is someone who will love me. I just have to find them.*

Angel put down the pen, then closed and locked the diary, moonglow sparkling off the tiny silver key. The candlelight by which she had been writing cast flickering shadows across her young, pretty face until a soft wind sighed through the meadow and extinguished the flame.

She leaned back against the trunk of the old oak tree and stared up into the starry sky. Somewhere beneath those diamond pinpricks of light, love awaited.

———

ACT II

TWO YEARS LATER...

Angel crouched in the corner of the alley as rats scurried around her, nosing through the rubbish. Laughter from the main street floated on the night breeze and something close to a smile ghosted across her lips as she was reminded of a time when she herself used to laugh, before her father stole her innocence. And then she remembered all she had lost, and the smile died, the laughter only amplifying her pain.

She raised the bottle of Jack Daniels—*Here's to you, Mom*—to her lips and felt it sear her throat. The booze burned when it hit her empty stomach. She hadn't eaten since yesterday, most of her money surrendered to her pimp, the rest purchasing the whiskey that now scorched her guts.

The last drops of liquor flowed down her gullet, yet she still slurped at the empty bottle, refusing to accept that her hollow solace was gone. She sucked air until she started hiccuping, then fired the bottle at a nearby rat. She missed, and the alley filled with the sound of shattering glass and jagged shards...

...flicked out...Angel stumbled back...forearm gashed and bleeding...

The memory was at once both ancient and fresh. Phantom pain flared in her arm. She grabbed at it with a gasp, fingers folding over the unsightly scars.

She had left home with just a battered satchel and a desperate dream, never once looking back, knowing only a loveless hell lurked behind her. She hitched rides with countless strangers until she finally reached Los Angeles. As she stood in the sun outside the truck stop, waving to the snuff-chewing rig driver as he returned to the endless highway, her heart had been full of hope. Surely here, in the City of Angels, salvation awaited.

Two months later, she made her first diary entry since running away from home.

Dear Diary,

I think I've found the secret to love.

Sex.

I've haunted the singles bars for two months now to no avail, watching the men approach the girls with the low-cut blouses and short skirts. Flesh sells, and I think if I want to find love, I must let men know that I'm ready, that I'm willing to love them any way they want if they'll just love me back...

She called home only once after running away, right after her first time. While not technically a virgin thanks to her father, it was the first time she had willingly offered herself to a man. She had been crushed when he was gone in the morning. But at least he had the decency to leave a note.

Angel,
Thanx 4 the fuck. Adios.

Angel's heart had been smashed to pieces under the iron hooves of her violated hopes. Eyes wet with tears, she picked up the phone and dialed home.

Her mom answered on the fourth ring—"H'llo?"—with her usual sodden slur.

Angel hung up. It was the last time she would ever hear her mother's voice.

Three months later she returned to the bars, hoping against hope to find someone who could heal the wounds left by a twisted father and drunken mother. But by then her belly was swelling from the bastard her father had sired, and men avoided her like she had leprosy instead of pregnancy. The disgust in their eyes drove her to do the unthinkable.

She would never forget the abortion.

Dear Diary,

I killed the one person in the world who would have loved me forever.

My child. My baby. My precious little Kristin.

If you can read these words from Heaven, child, please forgive me. While searching for my dreams, I murdered yours, and perhaps the hottest fires of Hell are reserved for such as me.

Can you forgive me, little one? Can you forgive me for having you torn apart? Can you forgive me for treating you like worthless trash? Dear God, make me barren for the rest of my life, for I never deserve the love of a child. Maybe I don't deserve love at all...

Nightmares followed the abortion, and she turned to the bottle to drive out the demons. Dead babies couldn't scream through a drunken stupor.

The whiskey blazed hot and heavy in her blood now, dulling her senses, making her drowsy. Her eyelids started to flicker like dying lights when a long, thin shadow reached down the dingy alley. Angel managed to keep her eyes open long enough to see a tall silhouette standing in the alley's entrance. Then the shadow moved, the *clop-clop-clop* of steady footsteps echoing off the walls as the dark stranger drew near.

Angel's survival instincts urged her to run, but her booze-slogged blood couldn't summon the energy. Her eyes flickered once, twice, then closed.

As she tumbled into numbing blackness, Angel felt strong but gentle hands slide beneath her. She had the vague sensation of being carried and then darkness enveloped her mind.

———

Reality...memories...the hellish void of a baby torn from her womb...a voice that would have cried "I love you, Mommy" silenced forever...

Angel awoke weeping.

Gentle fingers touched her cheek, brushing away the tears. A man leaned over her, smiling softly. "It's all right, child. No need to cry."

Angel's streetwise eyes studied the man. Middle-aged. Neatly trimmed red hair sprinkled with gray. Wise hazel eyes set in a face that managed to be both paternal and handsome, the subtle good looks marred only by a nose that curved sharply like a hawk's beak. But that flaw—if that's what you wanted to call it—was easily offset by his gentle smile.

But what Angel mostly noted was the clerical collar noosed around his neck. "You're a priest?"

His smile widened. "Are you asking me or telling me?"

"Just stating the obvious, I guess."

"The obvious must be stated sometimes. Otherwise, it stops being obvious."

"Obviously," Angel said, and they both laughed, tension broken.

"What's your name?" the priest asked.

"Angel."

"A fitting name for a gift from God. I'm Father Cochran. Or Mr. Cochran, if you don't believe in the Church."

"I don't," Angel confessed, then hurriedly added, "But I do believe in God." *Even if I think He's deaf.* She looked up at the priest, unaware of how fragile and vulnerable she appeared. "Why did you carry me here?"

"Finding lost souls like you is kind of my mission in life. It brings me great pleasure."

"But why me? Nobody cares about me."

Father Cochran put his hand over hers. "I care for you, Angel, because God cares. Who He loves, I love, and I want to show you that love."

Tears slid down Angel's face. "That's too good to be true."

"You don't believe in love?"

"I've never found it. And now I don't think I deserve it."

"Everyone deserves love, Angel. God even loves the devil."

"But I've...I've killed, Father."

"Who did you kill?"

"My baby." The two words sent spasms of agony through her soul.

"You had an abortion?"

It wasn't really a question, but Angel answered anyway. "Yes."

"Your sin has alienated you from God's love," said Cochran. "But there is a way to redemption." His fingers left her hand and slid up her arm.

"How?" But deep inside, Angel already knew.

Father Cochran breathed hot on her neck as his hand delved under her shirt. "Give yourself to me, Angel." His fingers glided across the smooth, flat expanse of her stomach. "Then I will say a prayer for your forgiveness." He unsnapped the button of her jeans. "You will find the love you crave." Her zipper slid down with a harsh rasp.

Moments later, they were both naked.

No, Daddy...

Angel closed her eyes as the priest crawled on top of her.

No, Daddy, please...

As Cochran drove his lust into her, a single tear scalded Angel's cheek.

No, Daddy, please don't...

———

ACT III

Angel sat under the welcoming boughs of the old oak tree. The grass was wet from the storm that had passed through this morning, but she didn't care. Where she was going, wet clothes wouldn't matter.

Clouds darkened the sky, but they were suffused with a golden glow, the sun blazing behind them, begging to break through. *How appropriate,* Angel mused. *The storm has passed, and now the sun will shine again.* She felt tears wanting to come but the gentle breeze whisked her face like a lover's caress, drying them before they crystallized. She looked down and read her final diary entry.

Dear Diary,

It's been a week since I gave myself to Father Cochran in the pitiful hope that the act would lead me to forgiveness for my sins and the love I so desperately seek. But Heaven's doors remain closed to me, sealed with the universe's biggest chain and padlock. I now know that what I have done is too horrid for simple absolution. The sacrifice must be greater if I am to find my salvation.

Nobody else—not my father, mother, my tricks, or even Cochran—robbed me of love. I stole it from myself. Though sired through sin, pure love was growing inside me, so sweet and innocent that it made even Heaven smile. And having this love, I let it go.

Angel looked up from the diary toward the sky. The clouds were still there, but the sun was definitely knocking on their door. Soon it would burst through and wash the meadow in gold. A soft smile on her lips, she took up her pen and began writing again.

I am damned. I'm not sure if there's a Heaven or Hell, but it's a risk I must take. There is no love for me here on earth and if Heaven exists, then I know my baby is there. I must go to her. If I cannot find love, perhaps I can at least find peace.

Dad, if you ever read this, know that I don't hate you. I did once, but I refuse to knock on Heaven's door with bitterness in my heart.

Mom, I followed your example. I pray you don't follow mine. But if you do, I'll see you soon.

Kristin, my precious little girl, I only hope that when I hold you again, I'll see forgiveness in your eyes.

And God, if You can hear me, I commit this one sin so that I can find absolution for another. Will you accept my sacrifice?

A single tear fell from Angel's eye and stained the page. She closed the diary and leaned it against the base of the tree. Only then did she insert the key and lock the book of secrets. She prayed the darkness and hell within those tear-stained pages would remain imprisoned there forever.

She flung the key far out into the grassy meadow.

The noose swayed seductively above her as she climbed the stepladder. As she slid the rope around her neck and tightened the knot, the wind sang through the leaves above, a sweet song of hope just for her. There were tears in her eyes and a smile on her face as a single ray of sun fractured the clouds and washed her face in a golden glow.

And then she spread her wings like a fallen angel and leaped into Heaven.

LOVE(?)

Your love cuts through my soul like a knife
Dark lies you whisper to my heart
Tears of pain I cry in the night

Your violent love has torn us apart
My heart is broken, my peace is shattered
Oh, how I wish for a brand-new start

You were the only one who really mattered
I mistook your hate for love
And your savage scorn for flatter

Your love was like a fiery dove
An angel from the depths of Hell
A demon from the heavens above

Your words of love were like a death knell
Your tenderness as soft as thorns
Your lust was for the bloody kill

A single look and our love was born
A single knife and my throat was torn

ALL THE WAY

AUTHOR'S NOTE

"All the Way" emerged from a dark place and time in my life, following the drugging and date-rape of a dear friend. In the aftermath, I screamed out an enraged prayer—Who the hell do You think You are? Nobody ever said prayers have to be pretty. I could not fathom why a supposedly all-loving God would let one of his faithful daughters suffer that kind of hell.

I received no definitive divine response, so I wrote "All the Way" as a catharsis. The theme of broken faith is presented and without much subtlety. I abstained from using a sledgehammer on readers, but neither did I use a feather.

I can feel his lips, hot and wet, nuzzling my neck. His tongue flicks out, more lizard-like than erotic, tasting my skin. Because it's expected of me, I throw my head back, offering my throat to his kisses. He takes my gift eagerly, almost clumsily, more like a fourteen-year-old boy in the midst of his first make-out session than a college sophomore with half a decade of sexual experience under his belt. The car windows have fogged up, and as he slurps at the nervous sweat pooling in the hollow of my throat, I watch rivulets run down the glass like tears. I suddenly feel the urge to use my finger to write EM PLEH in the condensation. Of course, no one passing by would really believe I needed help. People who visit this local lover's lane rarely want anyone to intrude on them, no matter what's scrawled on the steamed-up car windows, and I'm no exception.

I remember a night not so long ago, however, when I *did* want someone to help me, someone to hear my screams, even though I now know those screams were silent. But sometimes the soul screams louder than the tongue.

His hands grow bolder. Painful memories rise to the surface of my psyche, welling up like blood from an old wound torn open again, but I fight back the hurt and yield to his hungry caresses. I don't want him to touch me, but I know that letting myself be touched is the only path to healing.

I force myself to put my hand on his knee and then slide it up along his inner thigh. His breath is ragged in my ear, and I know he doesn't want me to stop. But I'm not ready. Soon, maybe. But not yet.

"Keep going," Mike says softly, then licks my earlobe.

He fumbles at my blouse buttons. I cover his neck with halfhearted kisses and hear him sigh with pleasure as my lips numbly dance over his skin. His fingers play with my hair for a moment, then grasp my open shirt and begin to peel it away. I tense, memories flooding back.

Relax, I scold myself, *it's Michael, and it's nothing he hasn't seen before.* Matter of fact, the only thing on my body that Michael has never seen is in my loose-fitting Levis. But it's there, hot and ready for him. It will be his before the night is over, because unless I give it to him, I can't begin to heal.

He senses my hesitation. "What's wrong?"

"Nothing," I assure him. "Just a chill."

"Well," he says with a devilish grin, "let me warm you up."

He crushes my lips lustfully, his tongue pushing awkwardly against mine as his hands stroke my thighs, caressing me through my jeans. But when he tries to reach between them, I shift position, denying him access. I'm not quite ready to give him that yet. "Easy," I murmur. "Good things come to those who wait."

"I've been waiting," Mike whines. "Do you know how long I've wanted you? How long I've wanted this?"

"We've been together before."

"Not like this. The last time was, you know...different." He shifts in the seat, clearly feeling awkward.

"Different," I echo. "Yeah, I guess that's one way of putting it."

"For what it's worth, I'm sorry about what happened."

"Let's move past it. After all, isn't that why we're here?" I give him a smile that I do not truly feel.

He looks visibly relieved. "I'm so glad to hear you say that. When you called tonight and said you wanted to see me again, that you wanted to take things all the way, I couldn't believe it."

"I do want to take things all the way." I take his face in my hands and stare into his eyes, repeating each word slowly for emphasis. "All. The. Way. Really, I do. I...I'm just not ready yet. Just go slow, okay? Here." I pull his T-shirt off over his head, baring his broad, muscular chest and washboard stomach. I lean over and cover the hard muscles with soft, fluttering kisses. I see the front of his pants bulge in response. "How's that?" I whisper, my tongue flicking out to taste the salt on his sweat-slicked skin.

"Great," he groans. His hands have easy access to my back, and I feel him unclasping my bra. The dark memories surge forward yet again, but this time I'm ready for them. I don't tense, don't hesitate, just help him peel the lacy garment away. It falls to the floor of the car. For some reason it looks sorrowful to me, like a piece of fallen moonlight.

I sit in detached silence as his hands and mouth find my breasts. The sweat feels strangely cold as it trickles down my body, but even stranger is the feeling at my core. I feel the seconds crawl into minutes. I'm almost ready. Almost ready to take the final step, to give him everything, to take things all the way.

Mike pulls himself away from my spit-drenched breasts and looks at me with raw need. "I'm ready," he says softly. "Please, I want you so bad."

"How bad?" I ask him, my hand gliding teasingly up the inside of my thigh. The lust in his eyes suddenly burns hotter.

"*Real* bad," he says, licking his lips.

My fingers touch my zipper. "Tell me how bad you want it."

"So bad I can taste it."

My voice is all honey and huskiness as I whisper, "If you're a good boy—or should I say, a *bad* boy—I might let you do just that." The car fills with the sound of rasping metal as I slowly unzip myself.

"Oh, yeah," he breathes, eyes sizzling with desire.

I reach inside. My own heat scalds my hand. My fingers slide between my legs and touch the secret there. The time has come. I want to give it to him. No, not want—*need*. I need to give it to him.

"C'mon." Mike sounds desperate. "Let me see it."

There is a harsh ripping noise as the electrical tape holding the small Smith & Wesson .380 automatic to my inner thigh tears loose. I shove the gun into Mike's shocked face. "Here it is, you sick bastard. Take a good look." Forget honey and huskiness. Raw venom now drips from my voice like venom from a viper's fangs.

Mike blinks like the stupid cow he is. "I don't get it."

"Come on, Mike," I say. "Did you really think I brought you all the way out here to screw you after what you did to me?"

"But I didn't do anything to you!"

"Really?" I lower my voice until it's nothing more than a wicked hiss. "You raped me, you son of a bitch. You raped the hell out of me even though I begged you —*begged you*—not to."

"You did not! You didn't say a word that night!"

"Because you drugged me. Maybe I wasn't screaming out loud, but trust me, Michael, I was screaming on the inside."

"I thought you wanted it."

It takes every fiber of my being to keep from pulling the trigger right here and now. "You liar," I say, spitting out the words like acid. "You *fucking* little liar. You were my best friend. I told you everything. You knew I was a virgin, knew I wanted to save myself until marriage. That was a vow I made to God and my parents a long, long time ago. But you took that, Michael. You took that away from me." I haven't blinked since I drew the gun. My eyes feel like desert sand, but I can't look away from him. Irrational or not, part of me believes that if I blink, he'll manage to disappear, to escape my vengeance. I can't let that happen, no matter how badly my eyes burn.

"You're going to shoot me for taking your virginity?" Mike says incredulously. "Isn't that a bit extreme? I mean, c'mon, being a twenty-year-old virgin isn't healthy. I did you a favor."

I can't believe the audacity of this piece of garbage. He's a sick fucking psychopath who needs serious professional help. Or a sick fucking dog who just needs to be put down. Hard to believe I thought I loved him once. "No, Michael," I say aloud, "I'm not going to kill you for taking my virginity. In time, I can probably get over that. I may have some scars, but I think I'll survive."

"Then for god's sake put the gun away!"

"No. Because what I *am* going to kill you for is taking my faith."

"Huh?"

"My faith, Michael."

"What the hell are you talking about? I didn't take your frigging faith."

"Yes, you did. Because of what you did to me, I

don't trust God anymore. How can I trust a God who lets sick shit happen to His children? I used to gaze up at Heaven and whisper 'I love You, Lord.' Now I look up there and ask Him just who the hell He thinks He is, who the hell gave Him the right to let this happen to me. And because of that, there's a big empty hole in my life, Michael, a big empty hole you helped put there. Love for God used to fill it, but now I hate Him, and because of that, I hate *you*."

"So stop hating Him! Maybe it's not His fault. Maybe the devil made me do it."

"I'm sure the devil *made* you do it, but God *let* it happen." I smile at him, but something in the set of my lips tells me the smile is ice cold. "Don't fret, Michael. I'll find my faith again. True believers always do. But you won't be around to see that day, because you'll be slow roasting in the pit of Hell."

"Please!" Desperation creeps into Mike's voice for the first time. "I'll do anything."

"You already proved that," I say. "Now take off your pants."

"Why? What are you going to do?"

"Just do it." I move the pistol an inch closer to his face. "And be quick. This thing's got a hair trigger."

"Oh god." Mike shucks out of his pants. Compared to his powerful chest, his legs seem kind of frail and thin. I hadn't really noticed that before, but then it's hard to pay attention to someone's legs when you're flat on your back, frozen and helpless, being violated.

"Shorts, too," I tell him.

"You want me *naked*?"

"You weren't bashful about showing me the goods a few months ago."

"That was different."

"Yeah, you mentioned that already." My voice is hard, uncompromising. "Take off your shorts or I'll shoot you in the guts."

Sweat rolls down his face, fear stains his eyes, and when he strips off his boxers, his manhood is a shriveled prune.

"My, my," I taunt. "Fear really does change a man."

"Please...don't hurt me."

"Sure, Mike, that'll work." The sarcasm rolls off my tongue like bitter honey. "Just like my begging *you* worked for me."

"You didn't say a word that night!"

"We've already covered this, Mike, and I hate reruns."

"*Please...*you can't do this."

I stroke the .380's trigger much the same way Mike stroked my body on that never-to-be-forgotten night three months ago. My thumb caresses the cold, deadly metal. "There are six bullets in this gun, Mike." I smile. "And every one of them has your name on it."

"Listen to me, I'll make it up to you." His words come out fast. "Just give me a chance."

Ahhhhh, the magic words. "A chance?" I echo. "You want a chance, Mike?"

"Yes, please, I'll do anything you want. *Anything.*"

"I'll give you a chance."

"Thank you, oh thank you so much, you won't regret this." His relief is almost comical.

"I'm sure I won't." I reach back inside my jeans and this time my hand emerges holding a scalpel. Moonlight pierces the fogged windows and glints along the ultra-sharp edge.

Mike's eyes, bloodshot with fear, open wide with worry. "What's that for?"

"It's for you, Mike. It's your chance to live."

"What...what are you talking about?"

"I'm going to aim this gun right between your eyes and count to five. If I reach five, Michael, I'm going to pull the trigger and send you straight to Hell." I hand him the scalpel, folding his clammy fingers around the handle to make sure he doesn't drop it. "But you have the power to stop me."

"Huh-huh-how d-d-do I d-d-do th-th-th-that?"

I point to the shriveled worm between his legs. "Just start cutting, Michael," I whisper. "Just start cutting."

"Oh my god...please...you can't..."

I touch the Smith & Wesson's muzzle to his forehead. "One."

"Please just listen to me!"

"Two."

"Will you just fucking listen!!"

"Three."

"For the love of God, please don't do this to me!!!"

"Four." I take up the trigger slack, the number five poised like the sweet taste of chocolate on the tip of my tongue...

...and then the wet sound of razored steel slicing through warm flesh fills the car...

...and Michael really begins to scream.

But hey, at least he's alive.

WORSE THAN DEATH

AUTHOR'S NOTE

I wrote this story in a single day at work when I was going through a zombie phase. The Walking Dead, the Dawn of the Dead remake, 28 Days Later—yes, I know, those aren't technically zombies— and a whole bunch of zombie novels, some good, most bad made me want to try my hand at the genre. With nothing more than a general idea of how I wanted to end the story, I started putting words on paper, and a few hours later, Worse Than Death was ready to be unleashed upon the world.

The baby's head exploded.

Russell Stavin jerked awake as wet fragments of infant skull bone splattered across the unforgiving walls of his subconscious. He dreamed the same dream every night, and it always ended the same way—with the baby girl's cranium blowing apart like a pome-granate stuffed with an M60 firecracker.

Except it wasn't a dream. It was a memory.

Reliving the memory every night when he went to sleep was his curse for the unpardonable sin he had committed as a USMC Scout Sniper in Afghanistan two years ago. The target was a high-value Taliban leader. The range was 900 yards. Not a gimme shot, but well within Stavin's advanced abilities. The window of opportunity was estimated to be only 10-15 seconds, with a second opportunity deemed to be low probability. Stavin and his spotter, Corporal Vincent Drake, lay motionless in their concealment for nearly twenty-two hours, patiently waiting for that narrow window to arrive.

When it did, the target was unexpectedly carrying his six-month-old daughter, the baby's head occupying the critical space between her father's head and the muzzle of Stavin's M40A3 sniper rifle. The Taliban leader's body was behind a wall, so there was no shot unless Stavin was willing to go through the infant to terminate the target. Stavin had refused.

Until Drake pulled his Beretta M9, screwed it against Stavin's temple, and explained to him in a hissed whisper that letting the Taliban leader live could result in hundreds or thousands of American deaths, and he would not let that happen on his watch, even if that meant sacrificing one Afghani brat. He took up the Beretta's trigger slack and warned Stavin that if the target exited the window of opportunity without a bullet in his head, then Drake was going to put one in his.

Stavin had mere seconds to make up his mind. And

in those seconds, took the coward's choice. Given the choice of eating a bullet himself or sending one down-range, he had pulled the trigger and fired a 7.62mm projectile into the baby girl's cherubic face at nearly 2,700 fps. The child's head simply detonated as the mushrooming bullet tore through the tiny skull and punched into the Taliban target as well, slamming into his temple and pretty much tearing away half his brain. The father-daughter corpses had collapsed into the dust.

Stavin waited until they had exfiltrated the area, then proceeded to beat the shit out of Drake. The spotter received a letter of commendation for assisting in the termination of a high-value target. Stavin received a dishonorable discharge for the assault and the curse of having to relive that kill every night. The nocturnal sequence was remorseless and unvarying.

Crosshairs locked on the baby's face.

Finger hesitating on the trigger.

Gun to his head.

Trigger pull.

Exploding cranium.

The jerking, gasping, shuddering return to consciousness.

His wife Abigail, God bless her soul, had proven to be long-suffering, patient, gentle. She woke with him, night after night, holding him close until the shaking subsided, letting his tears anoint her auburn curls, muffling his choked sobs against the crook of her neck so he wouldn't wake up their five-year-old daughter Britney in the adjoining room. She knew what he had done and loved him anyway. "For better or worse," she had said when he had confessed his sin to her for the first time, and she would never know how much her love and loyalty meant to him. When it all became too much to bear and his thoughts took a nasty turn in a dark direction, she was the lifeline that always pulled him back from the brink.

The only time that love had flinched was when she accompanied him to a counseling session, and he revealed that he sometimes thought about sucking on a gun barrel. Not just to end the everlasting nightmares, but as penance for what he had done.

In the car after that session, she had turned on him in something close to rage. For a second, he had thought she was going to slap him. Instead, with tears in her eyes, she had reminded him that he was not alone in this world, that even though he was in pain, he still had her and Britney. "You want to die?" she had snapped at him. "Do you have any idea how that makes me feel, how it would make your daughter feel if she knew? That we're not enough to make your life worth living." She had turned away, staring out the window. More quietly, but no less forcefully, she said, "You have plenty to live for, and don't you dare forget it."

It was the last time he talked about killing himself. He just sucked it up, learned to live with the pain, and went to sleep every night knowing he would kill that baby all over again. He crawled into bed night after night knowing that he would wake up screaming and that Abigail would be there to comfort him.

Except this time, she wasn't.

He rubbed the sleep from his eyes, then sat up and looked around. The light coming through the sliding glass doors was weak, the sun strangled by slate-colored clouds. Since he had dreamed of the dead baby again, he had expected it to be night, but the gray light indicated otherwise. He looked up at the clock hanging on the wall and saw that it was almost 1400 hours.

Wait a minute. Not only was it not nighttime, but he wasn't in his bed. He was lying on the dining room floor. What the—

He rose to his knees and listened intently. The house was still. There were sounds—the ticking of the clock, the hum of the refrigerator, the furnace kicking on to combat the late autumn cold—but the noises were mechanical, not human. Stavin knew, even without checking the other rooms, that he would not find Abigail sitting in the den reading the latest Jonathan Maberry book or find Britney curled up in bed napping with her favorite stuffed bunny. They weren't here.

He climbed to his feet and tried to recall the events leading up to his falling asleep or blacking out or whatever the hell had happened, but nothing came to him, not even a vague memory. He had no idea where his wife and daughter had gone.

He moved toward the front of the house, head pulsing painfully from a punishing migraine. No surprise there—migraines were one of his regular ailments, occurring with such ferocious frequency that his physician had prescribed emergency nasal sprays to combat the effects and prevent him from passing out. Now that he thought about it, that was probably why he had been sprawled on the dining room floor—he had been walloped by one of his without-warning migraines and blacked out. Wasn't the first time, wouldn't be the last.

He stepped into Britney's bedroom, navigating the

mountains of plush animals piled everywhere. The room featured a large bay window that looked out over their sloped front lawn and allowed him to see the entire length of their 500' driveway. Nestled on thirty acres of forested property in the Adirondack Mountains of upstate New York, they had built the house six years ago with privacy in mind, and the long driveway helped accomplish that goal.

It was only late October, but a light snow had fallen the night before. In the upper Adirondacks, the only month you could be assured you would not get snow was August, and even then, you wouldn't want to bet the bank. The white powder dusted the driveway, and Stavin saw tire tracks from a vehicle, presumably Abigail's Honda Pilot, cutting through the snow. No return tracks yet, so wherever she had gone, she was still there, Britney with her.

He was just about to turn away from the window when he glimpsed movement along the line of pine trees that rimmed the edge of his lawn, providing a natural privacy barrier between the house and State Route 3, a major east–west road connecting the widespread towns of the North Country. At first Stavin mistook the movement for a deer, but a moment later he realized it was their dog, a boxer-lab mix named Max. The dog had his nose down, snuffling along the trail of a snowshoe rabbit.

And then the dog died.

It happened so fast that it took a few seconds for Stavin to register what he was seeing. A man bolted from the tree line and tackled the dog like a lion taking down a gazelle. And then, as Stavin watched with horrified eyes, the man tore Max apart as if the dog was made of nothing more than wet paper. Even from fifty yards away inside the house, Stavin heard the anguished yelps of the family pet as the man ripped Max's front legs off and then used one of the severed limbs like a club to deliver a dazing blow to the dog's head. The man then buried his face into Max's throat.

What the hell is he doing? Stavin wondered.

His answer came a moment later as hot canine blood erupted in a sizzling spurt across the virgin white snow from the mangled hole the man had chewed in Max's neck.

As the dog shuddered with death spasms, the man clawed open the furry belly with bare hands. He pulled out greasy loops and slippery organs and shoveled them into his masticating mouth as fast as he could, seemingly consumed by ravenous hunger.

A gun, Stavin thought. *I need to get my gun in case that person or thing or whatever it is decides to make me the next entrée.*

He backed away slowly from the window, avoiding sudden movements that might attract the attention of the man currently feasting on the family dog. Once he retreated out of sight, he ran into the master bedroom and opened his gun locker.

Empty.

He stared into the voided interior for a moment, blinking in surprise as the black emptiness mocked him. He owned three handguns—a Taurus M44 revolver, a Taurus PT45 automatic, and a Walther P22 semi-auto—but they had all apparently pulled a Houdini and vanished from the safe in which he always kept them.

He grimaced as a fresh blast of pain zigzagged

through his brain and ricocheted around the inside of his skull like a berserk pinball. He bowed his head and rubbed his throbbing, migraine-afflicted temples. Where the hell were his guns?

The temple massage must have worked because he suddenly remembered that his father had his guns. Well, two of them anyway. His dad had taken up gunsmithing upon his retirement and liked to tinker with any firearms he could get his fingers on. The last time he had come up to visit, he had offered to make some modifications to Stavin's guns. He had taken the .44 Mag and the .22, leaving Stavin with the .45 so he would not be without a home defense weapon.

So where was it?

He began a room-to-room search and soon found the .45 lying on the dining room table next to an open gun-cleaning kit. Which made sense. He usually waited until Britney was absent before cleaning his guns, he and Abigail having agreed not to expose her to firearms until she was older.

The pieces of the puzzle began to connect. Abigail had gone into town with Britney to run this or that errand. Stavin had taken advantage of the alone time to clean his gun at the dining room table. The migraine had crashed down and knocked him out. He had awakened on the dining room floor, skull pounding as if a caged demon was inside using sledgehammers to try to break out of its bony prison.

And now there was somebody on his front lawn devouring his dog.

Stavin snatched the .45 off the table, retrieved a pair of binoculars they kept in a drawer for bird-watching purposes, and returned to Britney's bedroom. He again kept his movements slow and stealthy to avoid detection. The man was still there, kneeling amid Max's strewn remains like a blood-drenched supplicant worshipping an ancient god. His teeth still tore at mangled meat and sucked marrow from broken bones.

Stavin tucked the .45 into the waistband of his jeans at the small of his back and looked through the binoculars. He adjusted the focus until the face of the person eating his dog became crisp and clear. Even through the gore caking the man's features, Stavin recognized his nearest neighbor, a hermit-like recluse named Carl Dorset. The locals called him Crazy Carl because on the rare occasion he appeared in public, he was usually ranting about UFOs, government mind-control, and alien anal probes. He lived in a dilapidated camper on a junk-strewn acre of land adjoining Stavin's property.

Well, maybe "lived" was the wrong word...because Carl had died two weeks ago, his body buried in Union Cemetery, a mile up the road. Stavin had attended the service himself and watched the casket go in the ground. Looked like Crazy Carl hadn't stayed in the ground. Or in his casket, for that matter.

Through the binoculars, Stavin saw the grave-rot and death-decay on Carl's face as he continued his grisly feast. He still wore his burial clothes. But that didn't make any sense. Dead was dead...wasn't it? Stavin would sooner expect to see Max assaulted by a Sasquatch than by a dead man risen.

Recalling the ferocity with which Carl had pounced on the dog, Stavin knew he needed to warn Abigail and Britney. If they came home now, unaware of the threat lurking on their front lawn, they might be the next prey Carl attacked. Stavin could not allow that to happen.

Paternal instinct injected him with urgency, and he quickly spun away from the window to get to the phone, forgetting to move slow and not draw the attention of the thing that once was Carl. As Stavin hastily exited the bedroom, Carl lifted his head, blood dripping from his sunken jowls, and stared at him with eyes gone ash-white with the veil of death.

In the kitchen, Stavin finally noticed a Post-it Note stuck to the refrigerator door. He also saw that the message light was blinking on the answering machine. He grabbed the note first.

"Since you had a really bad night last night and finally seemed to be sleeping okay this morning, I didn't want to wake you. Britney and I are going down to Bloomingdale to get some groceries. Be back soon. Love, Abby."

Stavin's brow furrowed in confusion. He had been sleeping when they left? Surely she hadn't left him lying on the floor, so he must have been asleep in his bed. Why couldn't he remember waking up? He was showered, shaved, dressed, and had been cleaning his gun. He looked in the sink and sure enough, there was his coffee cup and cereal bowl, evidence that he had eaten breakfast. Why couldn't he remember any of that? He struggled for recollection, but all he did was make his migraine pound even worse.

Confused, he pressed Play on the answering machine. Abigail's terrified voice, barely more than a whisper, came from the speaker.

"Russell? Russ, are you there? Oh God, Russell, please pick up. I can't talk long. He doesn't know I have the cell phone. He's in the bathroom right now and...and he took

Britney. She's in there with him." A muffled sob. *"He has our baby girl, Russell. Damon Edgefield has our baby girl."*

Stavin's heart froze in his chest as if it had been dipped in liquid nitrogen. Damon Edgefield was a predator, a tall, scarecrow-thin scumbag who had served seventeen years in Ray Brook Federal Prison for the abduction, rape, and sodomy of a half dozen little girls in the Albany area. The only trait all the girls had in common was their age—five years old. During his trial, an unapologetic Edgefield had stated that he believed five years old to be "the perfect age to pluck the fruit of innocence."

The same age as Britney.

Edgefield now resided in a ramshackle shack on the outskirts of Bloomingdale and despite the townspeople's best efforts, he had refused to be driven off. He could be found in town on a near daily basis, buying beer and cigarettes in such quantities that you wondered where he got the money, given his unemployed status. Rumor was he acquired his income by selling kiddie porn over the internet, but nobody had been able to prove it.

Abigail's voice continued whispering from the machine. *"After we went to Norman's, Britney wanted to drive out to the marsh to see if there were any loons. The car broke down near Damon's place. I wasn't going to go there, but then these...these...things, like dead people, came after us. Oh god, Russell, it was horrible. They were covered in blood, and their eyes were white, and they made these terrible groaning sounds."*

Stavin couldn't believe what he was hearing. More dead people attacking the living? That meant Crazy

Carl wasn't an anomaly. This was happening other places as well.

"I barely got Britney out of the car, and the only place we had to go was Damon's. He let us in and shot all those people or things or whatever they are. But now he won't let us go. The way he keeps looking at Britney...and now he has her in the bathroom. Oh God! Britney's crying! He's coming out! I have to go."

The message ended with a beep that sounded like an alarm announcing the end of the world.

Heart pounding even harder than his head, Stavin went into the den, grabbed the remote, and turned on the TV. Every channel was running a breaking news special report; even Nickelodeon had stopped its endless cycle of *SpongeBob SquarePants* reruns to focus on the cataclysm gripping the world. Stavin learned the trivia of the apocalypse in snappy little soundbites.

"...the dead are coming back to life and eating human flesh..."

"...all major cities have been overrun..."

"...we have received word that London has fallen..."

"...the President has declared martial law..."

"...the cause of the plague is unknown..."

"...if they bite you, you will die, and then come back as one of them..."

"...no rhyme or reason. Some seem to be fast, some seem to be slow. Some seem to be mindless, others appear to be highly intelligent..."

"...the only way to kill them apparently is to destroy the brain..."

"...nobody seems to want to say the z-word, but it looks like a worldwide zombie apocalypse..."

Stavin leaned against the wall, stunned. It had

really happened. "The cause of the plague is unknown," one of the reporters had said, but right now the why and how were irrelevant. A covert military project slipped its leash. A black ops lab experiment spiraled out of control. The cleansing scourge of an angry God weary of wicked nations. Too many reality shows on television. Right now, the epidemic's trigger didn't matter, only surviving did. Maybe the survivors would one day have a reason to ask why, but with zombies swarming the globe, it looked like the survivors would be few.

Stavin gritted his teeth so hard that the enamel threatened to splinter. His fingers gripped the remote with equal force, and the plastic casing actually did crack under the white-knuckle pressure. He vowed that Abigail and Britney would be among those survivors.

He pictured Britney's precious little face...and then pictured that face screaming in the perverted clutches of Damon Edgefield. Rage, horror, and disgust ripped through him. He knew beyond any shadow of a doubt that when he reached Edgefield's house, he was going to tear him apart in a way that would make what Crazy Carl did to Max seem merciful by comparison.

Hold on, baby girl. Daddy's coming to get you.

The bay window in Britney's bedroom shattered.

Stavin quickly drew the .45 and edged cautiously down the hall until he could see into the bedroom. Crazy Carl—or rather, Crazy Carl's corpse—stood in the middle of the room, jaws moving with a clicking noise, eyes ash-white as they stared at Stavin. With a gurgling groan, the creature—*Just call it what it is, a zombie*—lurched at him. Its movements were swifter than he had expected. Stavin barely got the gun up before the zombie closed the gap, reaching fingers curled into claws.

Stavin registered the clumps of dog-flesh stuck under the zombie's nails a nanosecond before he triggered a triple-tap into its belly. The big bullets blasted chunks of rotting flesh into the air as they blew right through the ghoul. But it just kept coming.

Stavin retreated as the walking corpse lunged forward, fingers swiping dangerously close to his throat. At practically point-blank range, he put his next three shots into Carl's chest. More flesh went flying, along with fragments of his spine. But Carl could not have reacted less if he had been swatted with a cobweb.

"Why won't you fucking die?" Stavin snarled.

The zombie suddenly halted its attack and stood there, swaying, head cocked, staring at Stavin with those ash-white eyes. It seemed to be sizing him up. Stavin remembered the news report saying that some of the undead still retained intelligence. Maybe the zombified Carl was constructing a strategy in that dead head of his, coming up with a better way to take him down.

Stavin didn't plan on giving him another chance. Because he remembered something else the news report had said—"destroy the brain"—and realized he had wasted six rounds. He wouldn't waste anymore.

He raised the gun and slammed a round right between the zombie's white-veiled eyes. Those eyes vanished inside a soggy crater as the .45 slug drilled a hole through the skull and sucked everything in after it before exiting in an explosive red splatter. The zombie went down as if bitch-slapped by the hand of God.

The gun's slide locked back on an empty chamber.

The weapon took a seven-round magazine, plus one in the pipe, but apparently, he had not topped it off after cleaning it.

Stavin cursed. He was out of bullets for the .45. He had plenty for the .44 and .22, but they were at his father's. In the wake of New York's controversial SAFE Act, obtaining ammunition had become a real pain, and every time he stopped by the store to grab more boxes of .45 shells, they were out.

He was in the middle out of a worldwide zombie outbreak, his wife and daughter were being held prisoner by a sadistic pervert, and he was out of ammo for the only gun he had in the house. He'd been in some grim spots during his tours in the Middle East, but none grimmer than this.

Didn't matter. He was still going after Abigail and Britney. He would wage war with Heaven or Hell to save them, and since the undead were now slaughtering the living, it looked like Hell was actually sounding the call to battle.

He forced himself to pause and think, even though it hurt his pounding head to do so. As a Marine Scout Sniper, he was trained to evaluate the situation and plan for the mission before making a move. Just running headlong into a crisis without a plan of action was for civilians with no fighting experience.

He had to travel from his town to Bloomingdale, about a four-mile jaunt. Normally not a problem since Route 3 connected the two hamlets, but this was not a normal day. Once in Bloomingdale, it was a few miles on a secondary side road to reach Edgefield's shack.

It didn't matter if Edgefield had hurt Britney or not —Stavin planned on killing him just for even thinking about his daughter in that way. He should have done it a long time ago. If you're a shepherd with a helpless lamb, you don't wait for the wolf to strike before you take its life. You kill the wolf as soon as you see it to ensure the lamb is never harmed. Law or not, Stavin felt like his failure to end Edgefield's existence constituted a failure as a father. And now his daughter was paying the price.

Of course, she wasn't the first little girl to pay dearly for his mistakes.

The biggest obstacle Stavin could anticipate between here and Bloomingdale was Union Cemetery. The town was not large, but it had been here a long time, and there were a lot of bodies buried in that graveyard...bodies that would now be risen. And since the cemetery sprawled on each side of Route 3, that meant hordes of reanimated corpses clogging the road. A handful here and there, no big deal, just jump in the truck and run 'em down. But hundreds of zombies packed together would form a seething wall of undead flesh that would require something with more brawny horsepower than his Chevy Avalanche to plow through.

And then he remembered, recollection piercing through the pain in his head—his truck was ten miles away at Carcuzzi Automotive in Saranac Lake. A wheel bearing was going, and they had dropped it off yesterday to be fixed. So, he was without a truck, and Abigail had taken their only other vehicle, which was now broke down on the back road by Damon Edgefield's ramshackle hellhole.

Stavin went to the mudroom and opened the door to the garage, just to make sure. He confirmed that the first two bays were empty, but he spotted a backup plan sitting in the third bay.

His Honda Rubicon 500 four-wheeler.

In some ways it was superior to the truck. Better maneuverability, which might come in handy when weaving through a legion of the living dead. On the negative side, it could not offer the same level of protection afforded by a truck cab. Plus, it was much lighter, so if he hit any zombies with it, he was apt to damage the ATV just as much as he damaged the ghoul.

He could weigh the pros and cons all day, but it wasn't like he had a choice. The four-wheeler was the only means of transportation he had, so he would have to make do with it. He was going to get his wife and daughter, even if he had to pedal there on Britney's My Pretty Pony bicycle, complete with pink tassels and training wheels.

He studied the four-wheeler. Improvisation was required to compensate for the ATV's lack of protection. He needed some way to defend the Honda—and himself—when driving through the massed zombies he expected to find swarming the road by Union Cemetery. He also needed to find some sort of weapon. A bullet might be the easiest way to destroy a ghoul's brain, but it wasn't the only way.

He ran his gaze over the rack of tools on the wall beside the four-wheeler. Shovels, hoes, rakes, brooms... and a double-sided axe. And on the shelf next to the rack perched his three chainsaws. A plan began to formulate in his mind. He struggled to give it shape and coherency, but he finally managed to figure it out, though his migraine punished him for the mental effort.

But first things first. He went back inside and put on the heaviest clothes he could scrounge up. Steel-toed work boots. Insulated work pants. A thick sweater. A wool hunting coat. He finished the outfit off by wrapping a scarf around his neck. He knew none of it would save him if he was dragged down by a pack of the undead, but the layers of fabric might deflect one or two bites and gain him a few precious seconds. He suspected that when confronting flesh-eating ghouls, an extra two or three seconds might mean the difference between life and death...or rather, living death.

He deliberately tried not to think about Abigail and Britney and what might be—and probably was—happening to them right now. That would cause him to rush, and rushing would be a mistake. Part of a successful mission was taking the time to make the proper preparations, to attempt to predict every contingency and plan accordingly. The father in him just wanted to rev the four-wheeler down the road as fast as possible to get to Edgefield's shack. But the soldier side of him knew that if he did that, he would likely be killed by the walking dead and that would leave his wife and daughter at the mercy—or lack thereof—of a predator.

Urgency was understandable. Recklessness was not. And embarking on this rescue mission without preparing for what he would encounter would be reckless. Worse, it would be stupid. And stupid was not his style.

He kept the garage doors closed in case there were other zombies in the vicinity that might be attracted to the sound of him working. He then sawed the heads off the hoe, rake, and broom and sharpened the ends so that he had three long wooden stakes. He then used screws to attach them to the metal rack on the back of the four-wheeler so that they jutted out the rear like a trio of jousting lances.

Next, he touched up all the chainsaw teeth with a file and then filled the machines with the right mix of gas and oil. When they were topped off, he used a combination of bungee cords and ratchet straps to mount the chainsaws on the four-wheeler's front rack. He mounted one so that if pointed straight out in front of the ATV, another one so that it pointed off to the right and the last one pointed to the left. The ones on the left and right he turned on their sides so that the blades would act as motorized scythes.

When he got ready to go, he would fire up the chainsaws and use duct tape to hold the throttles open. Any zombies that attacked from the front or sides would be greeted with screaming chainsaw teeth. Anything attempting a rear assault would run into the sharpened wooden stakes. He studied his handiwork and nodded in satisfaction. As far as improvisation went, it wasn't half bad.

He grabbed the double-bladed axe off the wall and used the file to hone both edges before he used his last two bungee cords to strap it across the handlebars. He was just getting ready to start the chainsaws and hop on the four-wheeler when he heard the phone ringing inside the house.

He raced back inside and snatched the cordless phone out of its cradle. "Hello?" he said breathlessly, nearly panicked at the thought of what he might hear on the other end.

What he heard was Abigail's terrified whisper. "Russell, is that you?"

And then he heard something else, something that chilled him to the bone—the wailing screams of his daughter. They were muffled and distant, as if coming from another room, but they communicated her pain and terror with a raw clarity that curdled Stavin's soul.

Abigail was still whispering, so low he could barely make out her words. "Russell? Russell, if you can hear me, he did it again. He took her into his bedroom this time. I tried to stop him, but he hit me in the face with his gun. I...I think my nose is broken. Oh god, Russell, can you hear her screaming? I can't take it! Please, you have to do something! Please help us."

Britney's screams suddenly stopped, but Stavin could still hear her sobbing. And then he heard footsteps, followed by Damon Edgefield's voice bellowing, "What the hell are you doing? Is that a fucking phone? You fucking bitch, I'll—"

"Oh god!" Abigail whimpered. Then she began shouting, "Stay away from me! Stay away!"

Stavin heard the phone hit the floor, followed by the sounds of a scuffle. He nearly wept with the impotent frustration of being so far from his family when they needed him most. Britney's sobs and Abigail's screams and Edgefield's grunts coalesced into a violent, mocking symphony that concussed against his mind and threatened to shred his sanity.

"Honey?" he yelled into the phone. "Abby?"

Then he heard the distinct sound of flesh striking flesh and realized Edgefield had just punched or slapped his wife. She let out a sharp gasp that dissolved into sobs.

"Damon!" he roared into the phone.

He heard the sound of the phone being picked up, followed by the kind of heavy breathing that comes from either physical exertion or arousal. Clearly Edgefield was on the other end of the phone now.

"Damon, I promise you, no matter how many zombies I have to go through to do it, I'm going to kill you," Stavin rasped. "You hear me, you son of a bitch? I'm going to rip your fucking face off."

Damon chuckled. "Mr. Stavin, is that you? I want you to know, your baby girl is just about the sweetest thing I've ever—"

"Motherfucker!" Stavin snarled. "I'm coming for you."

Damon chuckled again, the sound like dry leaves whispering over crumbling tombstones. "Well then, sounds like I don't have anything to worry about. Buh-bye."

The phone went dead.

Blood frozen and head pounding, Stavin mad dashed back out into the garage, hitting the button to open the third bay door as he went by. The garage door rumbled up on its tracks and a few serpentine wisps of snow slithered in, blown by the light breeze that put an icy bite in the air. As he fired up the chainsaws and duct taped the throttle triggers wide open, he spotted a zombie standing down the hill, about fifty yards away where the driveway threaded through the row of pines. As soon as the ghoul saw Stavin, it charged up the driveway toward him. Just his luck, it was one of the fast ones.

He quickly straddled the ATV. Turned the key. Hit the starter button. The electronic ignition did its job, and the machine immediately rumbled to life. The charging zombie, decaying lips peeled from snapping teeth in a feral snarl, was only twenty yards away and closing fast.

Stavin slammed the automatic transmission into Drive and punched the throttle.

All four wheels grabbed the concrete and catapulted the machine forward. The zombie swarmed at him as if enraged its prey might escape its ravenous clutches, hellish groans coming from its death-rotted vocal cords.

Stavin tried to dodge around the zombie—no point in running into the thing if he didn't have to—but while the front chainsaw missed the ghoul, the one on the right side caught it just above the hipbone. The zombie spun away in a blur of blood, paying no mind as its chopped entrails spilled from the gaping wound.

As he sped down the driveway, Stavin glanced back. He recognized the ghoul as Mrs. Little, the preacher's wife from the Nazarene church on the edge of town. One of the sweetest souls you ever wanted to meet. She had died three weeks ago, and she most definitely did not deserve such a twisted fate. She deserved the heaven in which she believed, not the hell this world had become. He almost turned the four-wheeler around and went back to end her misery, but he just couldn't spare the time.

He had to get to Abigail and Britney.

He took a right turn out of his driveway and raced down Route 3 at forty-five mph. The revving engine merged with the roaring chainsaws to create an ear-punishing cacophony. He whipped past the gas station in the center of town and continued past the post office. He spotted a few zombies milling in the church parking lot like lost penitents, then a few more shambling around outside the local garage. Then the town's welcome sign flashed by on his right, and he could see Union Cemetery about a quarter mile up the road.

He eased off the throttle and let the four-wheeler coast to a stop.

It wasn't any worse than he had expected.

But it wasn't any better either.

There were hundreds of the undead massed in the middle of the road and spread thick on either side of it, a veritable sea of living-dead flesh, a wall of walking corpses. Drawn to the sound of the four-wheeler and the screaming chainsaws, the hungry hoard began to surge toward him, a seething, mangled mob unified in its swarming, hive-minded purpose of running him to ground and tearing him to pieces and shredding the meat from his bleeding bones.

Stavin quickly reconned the area, searching for a way around the zombie legions now churning toward him like a school of piranha, the fast ones taking the lead, the slower ones lagging behind. But their numbers were too great; when he factored in how difficult it would be to steer around all the gravestones, he knew he didn't have a choice.

He would have to go through the zombies.

The variance in speed between the runners and the lurchers worked to his advantage. As the putrescent pack drew near, their ranks were thinner, spread out. There was no reason, no logic, no tactic in this ravenous rush—only the instinct to kill and rend and devour. Had they remained massed together, they would have formed a nearly impenetrable barrier of undead bodies.

But spread out as they were, Stavin stood a sliver of a chance. Hell, maybe even two slivers. And he was damn sure going to give it a shot.

He slammed down the throttle. The gap between him and the zombies closed within seconds. They crashed together like warriors on an ancient battleground.

Stavin knew he could not afford to go off-road. He would be trapped among the tombstones, easy pickings for the zombies collapsing in on him like sharks drawn to chum. That meant his side-to-side maneuvering space was limited to the shoulders of the road. At first he tried to steer around the zombies and find spaces to drive between them. But as they crushed around him in a clutching, clawing, gnashing frenzy, he gave up and just gunned the four-wheeler straight ahead.

The chainsaws did their deadly work, carving a spewing, gushing, spurting swath through the undead hoard, mechanical scythes harvesting a field of fetid flesh. Blood and guts and gore stained the air crimson. Some of the zombies, dead for decades, were little more than skeletons; they flew apart like drop-sticks when the four-wheeler struck them, bones shattering like balsa wood.

Hands clutched at him. Nails clawed at his clothes. Mouths stretched wide, gaping voids of tooth and terror, brimming with the sounds of damnation. But all fell to the ripping blades. The knobby tires rolled and bumped and spun over fallen bodies. A wet spray of torn flesh and pulped entrails sprayed from beneath the wheels as Stavin rammed his way forward. Zombie blood sluiced him from every direction. Sodden chunks of ruptured meat peppered his face and clung with sticky tenacity. He ignored the gore and kept the throttle pinned wide open.

Time slowed to a crawl. His world became nothing but undead flesh and hungry growls and spurting fluids and screaming engines and tortured bodies and splitting organs and more endless bloodshed than he had seen in any combat zone. This was his life, his existence, his only reality. He was the epicenter of a zombie whirlwind and several eternities passed while he fought his way through the mass of monsters.

And then time ceased skipping gears and clicked back into its regular rhythm as he suddenly broke through the mob and saw the open road unfurled before him. He allowed a slight smile to tug the corner of his lips as he steered the gore-splattered ATV toward freedom.

Hell yeah, I made it!

He never saw the zombie that came from out of nowhere. The ghoul leaped at him in a flying football tackle from the right side, arcing its body over the chainsaw. The blow knocked him off the four-wheeler as if he'd taken a shotgun blast to the ribcage. As he fell, he instinctively threw out his arms, trying to find something—anything—to grab.

His left hand grabbed the chainsaw blade.

The merciless teeth cleaved through the meat and muscle in a split second. His fingers and most of his palm fell to the ground, leaving only his thumb attached. He felt the sickening sensation of the steel teeth ripping apart his hand, but no pain yet. Shock and fear and adrenaline kept it at bay.

He landed on his side as the ATV, with no one manning the throttle, rolled to a stop a few yards away.

The zombie crashed down on top of him, all snarling fury as its hands scrabbled at his thick clothing, trying to tear open his belly like a vault full of warm, tasty secrets. He used his right hand to punch the ghoul in the side of the head, sending it sprawling long enough for him to scramble to his feet.

Other zombies were closing in fast, driven mad by the scent of his blood. If he didn't finish this fight in the next ten seconds, he would be torn apart.

The zombie that had tackled him climbed to its feet and lunged forward with graceless, white-eyed hunger. Rather than retreat, Stavin stepped into the attack and slammed his arm across the ghoul's throat. The impact stopped the zombie in its tracks. Stavin then executed a leg-sweep that dumped the walking corpse on its back.

Stavin ran to the four-wheeler and quickly unstrapped one of the chainsaws—the one that had severed his fingers, as it turned out. He turned to see the zombie horde almost upon him. He was seconds away from becoming dinner for the undead.

Holding the chainsaw one-handed, the duct tape still keeping the throttle trigger wide open, he screamed, "C'mon, you maggot-breath motherfuckers!"

In unison, the zombies halted.

Stavin didn't know why they stopped and had no time to think about it. The same thing had happened when he had yelled at Crazy Carl. Apparently, something about his voice made the zombies hesitate. The zombie that had tackled him was still too close for comfort though, so he took two steps forward and shoved the chainsaw into its face.

The blade ripped through the sinus cavity. Brain

tissue sprayed in a chunky mess from the ravaged skull. The ghoul crumpled, and its own dead weight caused the chainsaw blade to chew its way out the top of its now-bisected head. Gore and gruel slopped everywhere.

Stavin held up the chainsaw and stared hard at the undead masses. "Anyone else want some?" he snarled.

They just stared back with those ash-white eyes. Their jaws continued to move in a gnashing motion, consumed with the need to devour, but none of them made a move in his direction.

Knowing he would never get the chainsaw mounted back on the four-wheeler with only one hand, Stavin hurled it into the motionless mob of monsters. One of the undead caught it right in the teeth and went down as if poleaxed.

And yet still the zombies made no move to attack. It was like spikes had been driven through their feet and into the ground, holding them in place.

Despite this fact, Stavin kept a wary eye on them as he climbed back on the idling ATV. Since he seemed to be in no imminent danger, he paused to examine his injury. The pain still hadn't kicked in—hooray for adrenaline, the all-natural anesthetic—and it wasn't bleeding as badly as he expected. He remembered hearing that when a limb is severed, the arteries automatically curl in on themselves to cut down on blood loss, one of nature's survival mechanisms. A tourniquet was still advised, but he didn't want to take the time. He needed to get to Abigail and Britney.

He pressed the shorn remains of his left hand against the front of his jacket to staunch the bleeding, then gunned the four-wheeler down the road, steering one-handed as he continued on his rescue mission. He glanced over his shoulder just once, long enough to see that the zombies had started moving again. But it was little more than aimless shuffling. None gave chase.

The need to both work the throttle and steer with one hand slowed Stavin's speed, but he still managed to keep the four-wheeler hustling down the highway at a steady twenty mph. He had to dodge around the occasional lone zombie, but nothing like the masses he had rock 'n' rolled—and chainsawed—his way through a few minutes ago.

The town of Bloomingdale was a quaint little Adirondack Mountain hamlet, complete with a school, church, two stores, a post office, a garage, and a population of only 1,350. As he rolled down Route 3 and crossed the Sumner Brook bridge, Stavin saw the town looked deserted. Either people had fled the area when news of the undead outbreak hit, or they were bunkered down in their homes. He spotted one zombie squatting in the snow-dusted parking lot of the courthouse eating the steaming innards out of a calico cat and another one pressed up against the front window of the Hex & Hop Brewery, but that was it.

Of the living, he saw no one.

He took the secondary road that jagged out of Bloomingdale and cut over to the town of Gabriels. The potholed pavement made one-handed steering difficult. All the bouncing and jarring threatened to dislodge the two remaining chainsaws from their straps. Stavin eased off the throttle. Better to go slow and arrive alive than to catch a pothole at high speed and go tumbling into a crash-and-burn. He would do his family no good if he ended up as roadkill.

Fifteen minutes and three miles later, he spotted Edgefield's cabin, set back off the road about fifty yards, entangled in thick brush and swampland. A miasma of desolation polluted the air, and the few stunted trees poking up from the rioting reeds on the front lawn failed to make things more hospitable. It was the kind of place nobody wanted to visit. The fact that it was the lair of a child predator just sealed the deal.

Two zombies—one male, one female—lurked outside the cabin. Both had been facing the front door as if waiting for it to open and grant them access to the warm prey they sensed inside, but when Stavin guided the ATV up the gravel driveway, the crunch of stones, rumbling engine, and revving chainsaws drew their attention.

As Stavin braked to a stop about twenty yards away, they moved in unison toward him. He spotted matching wedding bands on their fingers—a husband and wife zombie team who had apparently taken their "till death do us part" vows very seriously. The male brandished a baseball bat in his fist, which surprised Stavin. Sure, the news reports had said some of the undead were more intelligent than others, but this was the first time he had witnessed any evidence of that theory.

They advanced on him with a middling gait, neither fast nor slow, just a steady, relentless, forward motion. Their jaws clacked together in anticipation of fresh meat, their ash-white eyes fixated on their prey.

Stavin dismounted the four-wheeler and unstrapped the double-bladed axe. Wielding it with one hand, he swung it with all his strength in a sideways blow. It thudded into the female's head just above the ear. Skull bone crunched. The girl-ghoul went down, her status instantly upgraded from undead to just dead.

Stavin leveraged the axe out of her head just in time to find her partner nearly on top of him, swinging the baseball bat like Babe Ruth trying to knock it out of Yankee Stadium. Stavin dropped to his knees. The blow passed just over his head, close enough for him to feel the disruption of air as the bat narrowly missed scoring a homerun on his cranium.

The swing-and-miss caused the zombie to stumble off balance. Stavin thrust the axe-blade into the ghoul's ribcage. The impact sent the zombie sprawling in the weeds, the axe tearing free of the gaping gash as the creature fell.

Stavin scrambled to his feet.

So did the zombie.

Stavin was faster.

As the ghoul rose to its full height once again, Stavin was already bringing the axe over and down in a brutal, arcing, one-handed strike. The blade whacked into the top of the zombie's head and chopped open a gruesome wedge from crown to chin. The two halves fell away like split logs, gore slopping out to stain the snow crimson.

The zombie toppled. Stavin tried to pull the axe free as the ghoul went down, but the blade was jammed in thick bone. He cursed as the axe was wrenched from his grasp. He was reaching down to grab it again when he heard the scream from inside the cabin.

Britney's scream.

Full of all the horror and pain and fear a little girl can put in her voice.

Stavin left the axe stuck in the zombie's head and charged the front door. "Britney!" he shouted. "Daddy's here!" He grabbed the door handle. Locked. No surprise. They were in the middle of a zombie holocaust, Edgefield had taken prisoners, and he had known that one pissed off father and husband was on his way to rip his face off and beat him to death with it. So of course he had locked the door.

Stavin pounded helplessly against the unyielding wood. He could hear his daughter screaming on the other side, so close and yet so far, and those screams tore at his soul.

And then he remembered.

He had a four-wheeler.

And chainsaws.

Edgefield only had a wooden door.

Stavin dashed down the steps and climbed back on the ATV. He shoved it into Drive, aimed the machine at the front door, and gunned the throttle.

The four-wheeler raced up the porch steps like they were a ramp and launched into the air. The front chainsaw speared the wood and then the weight of the four-wheeler plus its forward thrust smashed apart the door in an explosion of splintered fragments.

As the ATV landed in a cloud of dust and debris, Stavin saw Edgefield standing against the far wall directly in front of him. A pump-action shotgun was pressed against his scrawny shoulder.

Stavin threw himself off the four-wheeler, but he was too late—the slug smashed into his stomach. As he suffered a skin-peeling skid across the floor, he glimpsed his wife and daughter huddled beneath a large mirror in the corner of the room. One of

Abigail's eyes was swollen shut, her nose a crushed mess smeared from cheek to cheek. Britney's clothes were torn to rags, and her face was bruised and bloody.

Stavin was consumed by a rage unlike any he had ever known.

Despite the smoking hole in his guts, he climbed to his feet with an inarticulate roar of primal fury and whirled on the man who had dared to abuse the ones he loved.

Damon Edgefield was impaled against the far wall by the four-wheeler and why he wasn't screaming in agony was a mystery to Stavin. The forward chainsaw had harpooned him right between the legs, the metallic teeth ripping apart his genitals into a pulpy mess that sprayed off the spinning blade like a crimson fan.

Rage infused Stavin with a strength he did not normally possess. He grabbed the back rack of the ATV with his good hand and pulled the machine away from Edgefield like it was made out of cotton. The child molester slumped to the floor, pelvis shattered, groin a raw, ravaged ruin. He was so thin that emaciation might not have been an inappropriate term. The crushed bones forged grotesque knots beneath his vaguely reptilian skin.

Despite the torturous agony he had to be suffering, Edgefield tried to raise the shotgun. Stavin knocked it out of his hands. It skidded across the floor and stopped next to where Abigail and Britney huddled in misery.

Edgefield slapped at him, but the blows were weak and ineffectual. Damon Edgefield was used to tormenting innocent little girls, not grappling with seasoned war veterans who had walked through hell and bore the scars to prove it.

Stavin crouched in front of Edgefield. "You touched my baby girl," he rasped. "You put your filthy hands on my daughter."

Edgefield's face was a mask of terror. "Get away from me!" he howled. Stavin saw tears in the man's eyes, but whether from pain or fear, he didn't know. Nor did he give a shit.

"I told you I was going to kill you," Stavin growled, his voice cold as a crypt. "And I'm a man who keeps his promises."

His hand shot out and grabbed Edgefield's lower jaw, his thumb hooking over the bottom teeth and sinking into the meat of the gums as his fingers dug under the chin, punching through the flesh and into the bone. With a savage snarl, he ripped the jaw loose and flung it away from him in a fury. Blood sheeted down the front of Edgefield's flannel shirt as his tongue flapped loose.

Stavin tore that off too. He threw it against the wall with a wet splat.

His prey silenced, he moved in for the kill.

He lunged forward and sank his teeth into Edgefield's throat. He felt the parchment-like skin part beneath his incisors and bit deeper until he felt the rush of air escaping a ruptured windpipe. A second later he found the jugular and relished the hot, salty spray of blood against his face as he burrowed deeper.

He tore apart the throat of the man who had hurt his family until Edgefield stopped thrashing. He then took one last mouthful of meat and gristle and pulled his head back. Skin and cartilage and veins and arteries stretched and snapped and popped, leaving nothing but a gruesome crater where Edgefield's throat had been.

And then Stavin began to chew.

He slowly rose to his feet, jaws moving, devouring the dripping mess he had torn from Edgefield's neck with his bare teeth. He swallowed, the raw meat tasting like a delicacy as it slid down his gullet. Then he turned and looked at his wife and daughter.

Abigail was on her feet.

Holding the shotgun.

Aimed right at his head.

Britney crouched and quivered behind her legs. She was looking at him in stark terror. Tears spilled down her cheeks, cutting tracks through the blood.

"Russell," Abigail whispered in horror. "What you have you done?"

Stavin looked in the mirror behind his wife and saw his reflection for the first time since waking up on the dining room floor.

His ash-white eyes stared back at him.

Memories tumbled through his mind in a jagged, chaotic rush of half-remembrances.

Sitting at the dining room table...cleaning his .45... weeping...thinking about the baby in Afghanistan...pressing the barrel to his chest, right over his heart...wanting to spare his wife and daughter the sight of a head shot...pulling the trigger...the bullet drilling through him...falling to the floor, dead within seconds...

Other things made sense now as well.

His inability to remember things...the pounding in his head...why the zombies stopped when he spoke... because he wasn't really speaking...he was just moaning and growling...they realized he was one of them...

I killed myself, he thought. *My God, Abigail, I just couldn't take it anymore. I'm so sorry.*

He turned to his wife and tried to turn that thought into words, holding out his arms toward her. "I'm sorry, Abby."

But of course, all she heard was ravenous, hungry snarls and saw two undead arms reaching for her and Britney.

Sobbing, she pulled the trigger.

Stavin's head exploded.

A LOOK AT: GATEWAYS TO ANNIHILATION: STORIES

BY JARRET KEENE

"Keene's collection is quietly magnificent. I can think of few things better than spending your time reading his words."

—Mercedes M. Yardley, two-time Bram Stoker Award-Winner

A cursed pizzeria. A haunted B-movie legacy. A tycoon's final robotic companion.

Welcome to *Gateways to Annihilation*—a searing collection of horror short stories that seamlessly fuses right-here-and-right-now themes of war trauma, pandemic stress, religious terrorism, political extremism, cryptozoological mania, and the human hunger for a sudden cleansing apocalypse, while encouraging readers to reach for a bag of movie popcorn in the darkness of the night.

Author Jarret Keene conjures 14 twisted tales where monsters lurk in neon shadows and infernal items hold lives hostage. Whether it's a Japanese war vet trapped inside Hollywood rubber suits, a Vegas comic shop owner stalked by satanic forces, or a billionaire's android nurse with sinister protocols, each story spirals into the uncanny with razor precision. In this collection that melds the nostalgic eeriness of *The Twilight Zone* with the nihilistic bite of *Black Mirror*, victims and perpetrators dance in blood-spattered loops of fate. Perfect for fans of weird fiction and supernatural thrillers, *Gateways to Annihilation* is literary horror with a cult heart.

AVAILABLE NOW

ABOUT THE AUTHOR

Mark Allen was raised by an ancient clan of ruthless ninjas—though breaking his oath of silence to say so might get him killed. When not practicing shuriken throws or hunting flea markets for a katana, Mark writes high-octane action fiction. He calls it "guns 'n' guts"—packed with twin Micro-Uzis, headshots galore, and punchy prose.

He wrote his first story at 16, won a regional contest soon after, and later published *The Assassin's Prayer*, which sold over 10,000 copies in its first year. Originally optioned by Showtime, the novel blends raw emotion with brutal action, earning Mark a loyal readership.

He lives in the Adirondacks with a skeptical wife, two martial arts–averse daughters, and enough firepower to keep door-to-door salesmen at bay.